I0684785

The Nostradamus Conspiracy

James G. Piatt

ISBN-13: 978-0-9859028-9-6
ISBN-10: 0985902892

Written by James G. Piatt

Published by Broken Publications
www.BrokenPublications.com

Edited & Formatted by Jennifer-Crystal Johnson
www.JenniferCrystalJohnson.com

A
Pacific Northwest
Publisher

www.BrokenPublications.com

Prologue

In these desperate and paranoid times of turmoil and chaos, most people are seeking answers behind the bedlam occurring in America and the world. Wars, terrorism, nuclear proliferation, the Arab Spring, and the warring factions of Israeli and Palestinian leaders have the citizens of the world questioning why.

Most people see tyrants or questionable government policies as the culprits. However, some groups state that most of these nefarious events are a conspiracy instigated by a few rich, powerful, and secret entities. Some of these groups consist of those who are called conspiracy theorists, known as 'the crazies' to most. However, some groups are made up of academicians that study such historical phenomena in depth. It is quite easy to disregard the conspiracy crazies, but not quite as easy to reject the learned opinions of professional researchers who, in many cases, have come to the same conclusions about conspiracies.

∞

One of the people caught up in a real conspiracy was Dr. Sarah Addison, a renowned archeologist who worked for the Archeology Archives Corporation. The corporation, a newly created firm with no experience in archeology, had mysteriously received tens of millions of dollars in no-bid contracts from the Department of Defense. This was at the same time that prestigious universities, who had always received grants in the past, were no longer receiving any monies.

Power brokers in high-level positions in the executive branch of the government who were associated with the corporation were also involved with a manuscript… possibly written by Nostradamus.

This story uncovers the truth about a strange conspiracy involving the Nostradamus manuscript, which mysteriously appeared in an archeological site in Sudan. The fulfilling of the

Nostradamus prophecies is critically important to a small group of wealthy and powerful people who will benefit financially from the chaos the fulfillment of the prophecies will bring.

Chapter One
The Archeology Archives Corporation

An executive from Germany created the Archeology Archives Corporation during the war in Iraq. His corporation was the result of direct ties to the conservative German chancellor who had a close relationship with the conservative president of the United States. The corporation received an infusion of tens of millions of dollars in no-bid contracts from the Department of Defense immediately after a call from the German chancellor to high-level people in America. This incredulous action stunned and displeased universities who had historically always been awarded the vast majority of grant monies for archeological endeavors. The grants had always been based on the specific university's background and past expertise in particular areas, as well as the experience and reputation of their professors of archeology.

The first no-bid contract given to the Archeology Archives Corporation called for locating and returning hundreds of Iraqi relics stolen from the Iraq Museum in Baghdad during the onset of the war.

The corporation needed a renowned expert in archeology and ancient Middle Eastern relics to head their archeology division and add authentication to their grant. After searching for months, they located Dr. Sarah Addison, a distinguished and esteemed site archeologist who had been working for one of the prestigious eastern universities that had lost their grant monies. She was called to interview for the position of Director of the Archeology Department in charge of all site excavations.

∞

Dr. Addison had no desire to work for a private corporation that appeared out of nowhere, had no historical credentials in archeological endeavors, and had siphoned off all government funds for archeological excavations, which normally belonged to distinguished universities. However, she had no choice if she wanted to keep working in ancient field sites. Her university, like most universities, was involved in drastic cost-cutting maneuvers and she had no hope of obtaining grants from within the university to pursue archeological digs in foreign countries. Since she was a full professor of archaeology, she could have remained the department head of archaeology and teach. However, in her heart she wanted to remain involved in on-site excavations, so she had taken a leave of absence instead.

She conveyed a timid demeanor, especially with her beautiful and innocent face. Her seemingly timid demeanor, soft brown eyes, short, curly auburn hair, and svelte physique gave her an edge in her interview for the position at the new corporation. Her scorching and intense passion when infuriated was a definite departure from her seemingly complacent character, but that was not revealed to her interviewers. She was unaware that their preference was pliability and a compliant team mentality before credentials and experience. Their main interest was obtaining an impressive name, not necessarily a highly qualified archeologist. However, with Dr. Addison they would get both.

∞

Dr. Addison preferred the academic atmosphere of the university to the corporate life filled with inane obligations associated with the primary goal of amassing money. She preferred musty, prehistoric ruins and hot, barren, sun-scorched dunes filled with ancient bones to wide, busy avenues filled with the frantic bustle of automobiles and the cacophony of a hectic, financially-oriented culture. She enjoyed the silent serenity of warm nights under huge, orange desert moons to the glaring neon lights of the metropolitan nightlife with its raucous murmurings and surrealistic, Ernst-painted existence.

She could have become a medical doctor, but considered the field too repressive and stifling. She opted to study anthropology, majoring in archaeology instead. Her studies mostly involved ancient Middle Eastern civilizations. She earned her Ph.D. at Columbia University in 1990. She had been actively working for a prestigious university excavating relics in Egypt and other Middle Eastern nations for 12 years when the grants vanished. She left her last field site when the United States government suddenly declined to further fund the university's excavations in the Sudan area.

The justification for the abrupt departure was stated in a formal letter to the university. It said it was due to unsafe and unstable conditions in the area as well as the dangerous civil upheaval. However, that had not stopped them from funding similar digs in the past when horrible atrocities were in full bloom and the conditions were much worse. It was a sudden, inexplicable, and disappointing state of affairs for Sarah.

∞

Dr. Francis Vachon, Sarah's new assistant director, was born on the outskirts of Paris into a middle class home. He was primarily a student engrossed in academics and the adult world. Being an introspective boy, he gravitated to science, history, and languages. He went to college at the University of Paris 1 (La Sorbonne) on a full scholarship and graduated at the top of his class. His undergraduate and master's degrees were in classical languages and ancient religions, and his Ph.D. concentrated on anthropology and antediluvian languages. He was offered a position at the university as an assistant professor immediately upon his graduation.

Francis had been a professor at the University of Paris for seven years and received his formal acceptance to a full professorship. He had a desire to be involved in onsite excavations to gain more experience in the hands-on areas of his studies. During the middle of his seventh year, he sent resumes off to universities who had received grants for such endeavors in the past. The universities sent back letters stating they had received no new grant monies for excavations and would not be hiring. He eventually sent his resume to a private corporation in

America that he had learned had received a substantial grant for archeological excavations in the Middle East and Africa. He was hired and took a sabbatical to take the position of Assistant Director at the corporation. He felt a few years in the world of field archaeology involving extensive onsite excavation work would be extremely interesting and financially beneficial. It would also add significantly to his knowledge of the most modern onsite excavation techniques. He knew of Dr. Sarah Addison and respected her renowned reputation and extensive experience. He was somewhat the opposite of her in that he was actually shy and had a reserved and ascetic comportment.

When it came to choosing between the hot, dusty, desolate, and barren sands of the desert and the colorful and lively avenues of the city, he preferred the city, especially the city of Paris. That was, of course, as long as he could escape to a comfortable classroom, an isolated and cluttered laboratory, or hidden stacks of books in a huge library when he became bored with the city's frenetic diversions. In many ways, he was similar to Sarah in that he loved the primordial world and its relics, ancient history, and especially the written and oral languages of ancient civilizations. He was slight of build and, though quite young, walked with a somewhat stooped gait, giving him the appearance of an aged academic professor of some ancient esoteric area of study… which he was, except for the age part. He had no idea that leaving his comfortable job at the university and accepting the lucrative, high-paying position at the corporation would bring extreme peril to his life, and possibly death.

∞

Although credentials were deemed important by the corporation to legitimize the receiving of government grants, it was Dr. Addison's mistakenly timid demeanor and Dr. Vachon's true reserved and mild manner that actually sealed their acceptance. The corporation wanted their people to be malleable, unquestioning, and corporation team members with all that it signified in the milieu of the corporation credo. The corporation, of course, had their reasons for wanting these traits, which were not necessarily ethical, as is true of many corporations.

∞

Dr. Addison's archeology team was sent to Iraq and eventually salvaged about 65% of the stolen Iraqi museum relics. They brought them back to corporate headquarters to be analyzed and cataloged before turning them over to the government, who would return them to the Iraqi museum authorities through the proper diplomatic channels. At least that was what was assumed in Dr. Addison's mind.

An uncommonly rare and extremely problematic event occurred directly after the priceless artifacts were brought back to the corporation's archeology laboratory. While the archeological team was away over a long five-day paid holiday, the corporation seized the artifacts. When Dr. Addison returned to work, she discovered they were missing from her laboratory. The taking of the relics on the part of the corporation was something completely out of the ordinary, as well as an unthinkable and unethical practice in academic circles.

Dr. Addison, much to the astonishment of other team-oriented, obsequious mid-level managers, vociferously questioned the intention and breach of ethical practices of the corporation for taking the relics. She demanded with red hair flaming and brown eyes flashing that the artifacts be returned immediately to the anthropology laboratory so she and her team could finish the job. Not satisfied with the evasive and non-committal bureaucratic answers she had received from intermediate managers, she demanded to see Horace Coopman, the vice president of procurements, to register her complaint in person.

This event was a foreshadowing of future ominous events that would eventually place Dr. Addison's life and the lives of others in extreme danger. The result of the event would send her on perilous journeys into the mountains north of San Francisco, the shadows of the Vatican in Rome, a kindly professor's cottage in the hills of Rome, and a secret underground FEMA city-base miles deep in the ground near the town of Santa Rosa, California.

∞

At the meeting with Horace, she was told in an extremely brusque manner not to question the decisions of the corporation that did not concern her.

She glared at him with her red curls bouncing.

"Mr. Coopman, all artifacts found *are* of my concern and are the property of my department until we are finished with them."

He sneered, shook his head, and pointed at her face harshly with a large finger.

"The artifacts are not yours and were never yours, Dr. Addison. The artifacts were always the temporary property of the corporation, and we did with them what we desired." Then, with a malicious glare, he said, "You are no longer in the lofty hallowed halls of academia. You are now in the adult world and you had better grow up if you wish to stay employed here!"

Her face flamed, eyes flaring as she started to argue.

"I have never been treated so poorly or seen such flagrant abuse of protocol! You can't—"

He interrupted her sputtering rudely.

"The recovered relics from Iraq are already on their way to the Iraqi museum per the defense department contract and your request is not only unjustifiable, but not even possible now. It's too bad that you feel you have been treated poorly, Dr. Addison, but you must understand that we are a private corporation and not an ivory-towered university. You are an employee hired under a contract without any timed duration. In other words, your time at the corporation is subject to our will. You don't get tenure in the real world, our corporate world!"

He told her that Iraqi museum archeologists would complete the analysis and categorization of the relics in Iraq. Dr. Addison had never in all her years of managing excavations for universities run against such an outright and flagrant misuse of authority and breach of archeological ethical practices.

She said irately, "The suppressing of accepted protocols on the corporation's part is totally unacceptable, Mr. Coopman!"

He laughed at her in a hostile manner. "This meeting is over. I would advise you to gather your temper together or you will find yourself being replaced."

Lost for words, she shook her head and stomped out of the office, her face as red as her hair. She thought about quitting on the spot but knew she couldn't because she had too much invested. She didn't want to go back and teach at the university, at least not now. In the back of her mind, she thought naively that things could get better in the future. She was very wrong on that crucial point and, in fact, they would worsen tremendously in the future.

After the uncomfortable situation concerning the Iraqi relics, Francis, Sarah, and some of her team were immediately sent overseas to different countries in Europe and the Middle East. It was the corporation's way of keeping them conveniently away from corporation headquarters. They would be on various archaeological sites for almost three years.

∞

Maximilian Vogel, the CEO of the Archeology Archives Corporation, summoned Sarah to his office after the team had come back to California. When Sarah entered the ostentatious office furnished with opulent antique furniture and priceless relics, the huge, gruff-looking German CEO in a dark gray cashmere suit rose from behind his antique mahogany partnership desk. He nodded slightly as he shook her hand and spoke in broken English.

"Dr. Addison, I have a new and very important assignment for you and your team. We have just received a lucrative contract from the federal government to do archaeological excavations in a portion of Sudan that was once part of the ancient Nubian Empire. I know that you have had extensive onsite experience in that region and are very familiar with the area. I know the archaeological tasks you have had overseas for the past years have been somewhat lackluster to what you desire, but I am sure this one will be quite fulfilling. I want you to get your team outfitted and ready to leave by next week. The excavation could last up to three months."

"That is excellent news, Mr. Vogel. Has the general site area been located so we can do a walk-through of the surrounding area? What will we be looking for specifically?" Dr. Addison asked, showing her interest in the proposal.

"The engineering branch of the defense department already used what they said is an exotic, newly designed infrared system to develop a comprehensive set of aerial photographs of the exact area. It was completed a few months ago. I will have all of that data including the aerial photography and topographic maps with the site delineated ready for you by tomorrow."

"I see… I guess then all we will need to do is use a Global Positioning System to help us determine precise locations obtained from the aerial photos. Once we get there, we can use ground-penetrating radar to help us reveal any deeply buried structures or graves."

"Yes, yes, that is all fine. It is up to you as to what you do and what equipment you need to perform the excavations." He hesitated, looked out the window, and then said, "As to the specifics of which the government has an interest, they are indistinct. However, everything you locate at the excavation site should be deemed of critical importance. Therefore, all artifacts must be categorized and sent back to headquarters at the end of each week. I hope you understand the importance of that! Your team can analyze the artifacts thoroughly once you return to headquarters. We do know that the government is particularly interested in anything from the ancient fourth or fifth century Nubian culture. Any relics from that period should be considered of extreme importance."

Sarah almost questioned him more about the excavation, being suspicious with the fact that the precise area had already been outlined, but instead just nodded her head. As she was about to leave, she noticed a particular relic displayed in a glass case in the far corner of the office. She squinted her eyes and shuddered. She recognized the piece and was reminded of her first unpleasant experience with the corporation in regard to the stolen Iraqi relics. One of the original priceless Iraqi museum relics her team had brought back sat on a pale red satin pillow atop a golden base. Maximilian Vogel had it unabashedly displayed in a glass case, with several tiers of glass containing other relics, standing prominently in one corner of his office. She wondered how he had acquired them and under what authorization. She had a suspicion it might have been done unethically, if not illegally.

She gazed questioningly at the huge man for a few seconds, held her temper in check for once and said, "That will be fine, Mr. Vogel. We will send everything back each Monday. You'll make sure that we have all relics stored in our laboratory storage room to analyze and categorize after we get back then?" She stared at him, hinting that she was questioning whether the items would be there when she returned.

"Yes, of course. Why wouldn't they be here?" Max stated irritably in his brusque German accent. He then rudely turned around and looked out the window, raising his hand in dismissal without allowing her to see the convulsive tic that was taking place in his left eye now. He had not expected her to question his integrity or that of the corporation, and his irritation was revealing itself openly.

Sarah felt a chilly finger tracing a long-healed childhood scar down the nape of her neck and shivered as she stared at the menacing silhouette of the huge man's back outlined by the afternoon light beaming through the window. She left without any further questions. After the incident with the Iraqi artifacts, she had no faith in the integrity of the company and now, after seeing one of the stolen Iraqi treasures as well as other priceless artifacts in his opulent office, she did not trust the CEO himself.

∞

She left the office and walked down the hall. She couldn't

understand why the corporation continually received a vast majority of the lucrative government contracts for onsite excavations. The universities that had such grants in the past now rarely received any, and when they did get a contract, it was always for a short duration.

She thought about the new task and sensed it was very odd that he wouldn't tell her for what they were searching. She was sure the government agency that gave the contract to the corporation knew exactly what they were after, and that was why the site location had already been surveyed aerially. That fact didn't take a brain surgeon to ascertain. All of the other site excavations for the corporation during the past years required normal walk-throughs and traditional site mapping methodology as well as knowledge of the things for which they were searching.

She had the same feeling in her stomach she'd had when her team had the stolen Iraqi artifacts taken away prior to the completion of their job. She knew that something was definitely wrong. Her mind wandered back to the priceless relic in the CEO's office and she wondered how many stolen relics had actually been returned to the Iraqi museum. She also wondered how many relics from past excavations had been kept from the government, a government whose oversight was historically poor in these areas. She speculated about how many of the other top executives in the corporation had priceless relics sitting in elaborate glass cases in their offices, or even in their homes. After this assignment, she promised herself that she would quit and accept the position as a teaching professor of archeology at her university.

The excitement of a new excavation in an area for which she longed to visit again ultimately took dominion over her angry and questioning suspicions and her temper slowly drained away. She thought out loud to herself as she walked down the hall, away from the luxurious office.

"I wonder if the relics had been there long before the brief and bitter discourtesy which rebuked me as the lowliest born? Oh, Sarah, you must learn to take things less seriously! Does my search for honesty give a rightful birth to my incessant desire to unearth endless injustices? I could continue all my life to fight for what I perceive as injustices without hearing others who have their own perceptions, which could be just as authentic. My heart, what needs it to beat if nothing but my own causes are considered sweet?" She shook her head sadly, dismissed her dark thoughts, and walked quickly back to the lab to discuss the new task with Francis and the team.

∞

When she finished telling Dr. Vachon about the Department of Defense's repeated involvement in an excavation, he shook his head.

"Once again, we have the corporation involved in a major multimillion dollar contract for excavating a site. To make things worse, this time the excavation site has already been surveyed by the Department of Defense. I just don't like it, Sarah! Don't you feel the whole thing is a little odd? Why is the Pentagon funding this particular excavation project? What do they expect us to find in the desert? They must know or they wouldn't have the site already outlined in such detail for us!"

"I feel it is quite odd, too, Francis, especially since the exact location has already been specified by the Pentagon. This time we will have to be much more circumspect about what we do and say. By the way, Mr. Vogler is even more contentious and arrogant than Mr. Coopman. I don't care for either of them, nor do I trust them. Mr. Vogler has one of the precious stolen Iraqi treasures we located years ago in a glass case in his office."

"*Ce qui? Vous doivent-il me badiner, comment pourrait-il cela?*" Francis sputtered in French; he was so upset. "Shouldn't you tell someone, the government perhaps?" he asked naively.

"I don't think it would do any good since someone in the government was the one who took the relics from the corporation to give back to the Iraqi museum in the first place. Francis, I sometimes think I need to stop being so suspicious and high-minded. My negative outburst may be affecting you. Maybe there is a legitimate explanation for all of this. Perhaps in the last situation involving the Iraqi stolen relics, the Iraqi government *gave* it to the corporation president as a gift for finding hundreds of their precious treasures. Anyway, we don't have time to worry about it now; we need to get ready for our new excavation assignment. I am excited about getting back to the Sudan! You will love it there!"

"Yes, but of course, Sarah. I will make up a list of all the things we will require, then inform the team, and start to get everything packed and ready to go. I'll check in with you later if we need any equipment."

She nodded and then frowned as she contemplated the strange scenario again. She did not feel encouraged about another excavation funded by the Department of Defense. In fact, for some reason she had a cold dread about it this time and she couldn't shake it even with her newly open-minded attitude.

Little did she realize at the time that her worst fears would become a reality. Eventually, corporation and covert CIA agents from the Department of Defense would hunt her and Francis down over what they would find at the excavation site in the Sudan. Eventually, their lives and the lives of others would be placed in peril and they would be forced to flee.

∞

After his meeting with Dr. Addison, Maximilian Vogler was talking to a man on the phone.

"Yes, our archaeology team will be leaving by the end of the week. No, I didn't say anything about what we expected them to find; Dr. Addison has a suspicious mind and is asking too many questions already. Do you think the articles were planted deep enough and placed correctly to satisfy her? ... Yes, I see, I suppose that will be adequate. Six months should give the land enough time to get back to its original state. Yes, we will send you the items as soon as they are sent back to us.... What? ... Yes, one of our security officers has been added to her team to keep track of everything that is found at the site.... Yes, he will be making a list of every relic found and will be in charge of packing them to send them back to us each week." Max was going to ask why the objects were so important this time, but he didn't. He never questioned the ethics or intentions of Darren Williams, the personal counsel to the President of the United States. Besides, he really didn't give a damn about reasons, just as long as he got his money. To him – in the Ayn Rand tradition – whatever made him wealthy was moral and ethical.

During the next five days, the archaeology team purchased a few new pieces of equipment and amassed all of the other gear they had in their laboratory that they would need for the months ahead in the harsh desert conditions of the Sudan. Dr. Addison and Dr. Vachon researched the area in which they would be digging to determine what might be of interest to the corporation, and especially to the Department of Defense. They came up with no logical answers, only 50 or so pyramids, which could hold some important relics.

They were given one new person who would be in charge of the relics when they were unearthed and would do the packing for their return to the corporation. Sarah knew there was no need for him, especially since he did not have any qualifications for onsite fieldwork. It made her feel uncomfortable, especially since he was put in charge of cataloging the relics. She told Francis and one of her trusted team members to keep a watch on the new man and be aware of anything important he might do that was out of the ordinary.

Sarah wondered how the government was able to give a grant to the corporation to go into the same area where her university had lost an excavation contract many years ago, when the conditions were even worse now than they were then. The whole situation was an enigma to her. Her feelings of dread were enhanced by the new adventure, but she couldn't say why.

Chapter Two
The Nubian Excavation Site

The plane transporting Dr. Addison's team flew over an area in Sudan where the Kushite kings had once traveled south to the Sudanese savannah to build a capitol at Meroe. At the end of the fourth millennium BC, Egyptian culture influenced the Nubian peoples, but eventually the traditions of the black kings prevailed over the cultural heritage of Egypt.

A large temple complex called the Great Enclosure was just south of Meroe near the Sixth Cataract. Some religious historians stated that this area was possibly the original Garden of Eden, instead of the area along the Tigris and Euphrates rivers as attested by most Christian historians. Of course, the logical and pragmatic Catholics stated the Garden of Eden was only a metaphor that expressed a certain moral concept, anyway, so its actual location was not in either setting. Sarah figured they were probably right. Fundamentalist Protestants believed the biblical story word for word, even the apple part! She wondered why the fundamentalists even ate apples, since that was supposedly what got Adam and Eve thrown out of the garden. She then pinched herself for being so ungenerous.

Eventually, a combination of religious beliefs affected the Nubian culture and Kush arose. It was created by the beliefs of Egypt to the north and those of African peoples to the south. Kush, however, was not to last. As soon as the kings of Kush established their rule from Abu Hamad to the Nile Delta, the Assyrians came in and defeated their armies. By the year 654, the Kushites had been driven back to Nubia and the security of their capital, Napata. Although reduced from a respected power to a small remote sovereignty, Kush continued to rule over the middle Nile for another thousand years with its unique Egyptian-Nubian culture and gifts of prophecy intact.

The Kushites established their own language, which was eventually developed into a unique cursive script. It was reported through the ages that the Nubian Kushite mystics wrote prophecies using the cursive script. Esoteric prophecies of the future, it was rumored, were hidden in secret scrolls, but few were ever reported as being found, so the rumors remained just that for the most part. Dr. Addison and Dr. Vachon would have the unique and exciting opportunity to view the esoteric written language detailing such prophecies firsthand in the months to come. The scroll of Nubian-Kush prophecies they would find would be seen for the first time since they had been written, or so they thought. Those findings would be the start of a perilous journey into danger.

∞

Francis, sitting in the back of the plane with the rest of the team, gazed pensively down upon the savage burning sand of the Sudan, remembering something from his past studies.

"And their passing away shall have no authority under the windings of the burning sand and they – lingering motionless in the scorching silica covering the desert – would not die easily but would twist on racks of heat until ligaments gave way, revealing their pure white bones."

"My god, Francis, what was that all about?" one of the team members overhearing his dark musings asked.

"Oh, sorry…. I was just philosophizing out loud about the dead black pharaohs of the Kushite Dynasty and of their burial pyramids and the blistering sands in Nubia, where we are going and they were buried. The number of pyramids in Nubia, totaling nearly 223, far exceeds the number found in Egypt, you know. There are over 50 ancient pyramids and royal tombs in the desert sands just around Meroe alone, which is our destination. They are Africa's best-kept secrets… it is quite fortuitous that we were allowed to excavate in the area." The team did not know, nor did he make them aware, that it was of deliberate design by the Department of Defense and anything but a fortuitous event. "We will probably, along with many very important artifacts, find those white bones of the black pharaohs of which I spoke."

"Is there still a religious group in existence today that was once affiliated with the black pharaohs? I had read somewhere that such a religious entity still exists."

"I am not sure if the identical religion is still in existence, but there is bound to be some ancient religious group relating back to that of the black pharaohs." Little did Francis know at the time that a religious group whose existence dated back to those early times of the Kushite Dynasty would play an important role in his and Sarah's destiny.

∞

After digging in the sand for over nine months at the Sudan excavation site, hundreds of pieces of ancient Kushite and Egyptian relics had been unearthed along with countless Nubian artifacts and shards. Many white bones, as predicted by Dr. Vachon, had also been found, cataloged, and packaged for shipping. The relics had been located in the 260 meters by 280 meters by five meters deep area that had been initially outlined by aerial photographs and further delineated by GPS and ground piercing radar. The area was now outlined with ropes tied to sticks stuck in the sand.

Dr. Sarah Addison, digging in a new area near the ruins of one of the pyramids, was carving out a buried artifact with a trowel and paintbrush. A piece of green material suddenly protruded from the hard, baked, sandpaper-like soil. A large green gem gleamed into full view as she continued dusting the sand from around the artifact. She stared at the object once it was partially unearthed and took in a gulp of air as she slowly and meticulously dusted away the rest of the yellow sand. She frowned, thinking that normally the sand should have been much harder around the amulet, but let the question sink into her subconscious as she dusted away the rest of the dirt from the shiny green object.

She glanced over to see if any of the team members were watching, especially the one that had been assigned by the corporation. She saw that everyone except she and Francis had left the area and gone back to the camp to categorize, list, and pack the finds for the day.

∞

Yesterday evening, Francis had been working near a crumbled wall after digging a trench in front of the same pyramid and extending the trench into the ground next to the wall. He had unearthed a large Meroitic earthen jar. No one had seen him; he surreptitiously placed a sack over it and carried it over to Sarah. He gave her a glimpse of an ancient scroll and a manuscript inside. They covered it back up with a small hemp sack and hid it in a hole near the pyramid until they could bring it safely to their tent without others seeing it. Finding the relics in the large earthen jar was why Sarah started digging near the same area the next day.

That night when they inspected the contents of the jar, they found what they believed to be an ancient Nubian scroll and a more modern manuscript. Francis determined that while the scroll was written in a straightforward Kushite script dating to the fourth or fifth century, the verses in the manuscript were modern and were written in an ambiguous style with a mixed vocabulary consisting of classical French, Italian, Greek, Provencal, and Latin. He told Sarah that Michel de Nostradamus was the only one that he knew who used that peculiar and obscure style. He said it had been used primarily to avoid his being prosecuted as a magician and subject to trial for heresy by the Catholic Church.

Francis sighed. "Nostradamus also, calculatingly, confused the time progression of his prophecies so that their secrets could not be revealed by anyone except the professionals trained by him. A major problem came into existence later when he and the professionals who he had trained all died. They left without leaving any clues about how to accurately translate the prophecies or the method for determining the timelines of the verses."

"You feel the manuscript could be written by Nostradamus."

"Yes, I believe it may have been. There is another peculiar thing here, too: one short sentence in the Nubian scroll that we have gone over for about three hours appears to be similar to a sentence we found in the Nostradamus manuscript."

"Yes, I agree. The manuscript and scroll's sentences appear to be analogous in content as well as context. This is extremely odd!"

Even though their enthusiasm was at a climax, they kept the information to themselves so that the new member of the team would not know.

∞

When Dr. Addison got through dusting the sand from around the green artifact, which was about four centimeters in depth and almost eight centimeters in diameter, she carefully lifted it and found it was a green stone amulet with a heavy 24-carat solid gold-laced chain attached to it. She gasped then quickly looked around to see if any of the others had come back and witnessed her finding the artifact. Not seeing anyone, she whispered over to Francis, who was digging a few meters away.

"Francis, come over here!" She also put her finger up to her lips to denote silence.

Francis looked around surreptitiously, walked casually over to Sarah, and sat on his haunches. Sarah showed him the emerald green artifact.

"Oh, my god!" he remarked.

"The green stone amulet has cursive writing on the front and the back. It also has a tiny etching of an image with the head of an ibis and the number 1700, as well as writings on the back. Do you have any knowledge of such a thing?"

Francis took the amulet in his hand, and in a low voice hardly controlling his enthusiasm said, "My god, this could be it, Sarah. It could be the key that was written long ago by experts concerning the solution to translating the Kushite scrolls of prophesies. It was also written according to some historians that one of the mysterious emerald amulets of Thoth would be the key to the true translations of the Nostradamus prophecies as well as the Nubian scroll. The newer manuscript that I found most assuredly could be one of Nostradamus' last writings and just possibly this green amulet is the key of which they spoke for translating his prophecies accurately. We could use it to go over the sentences of both the scroll and the manuscript we translated the other night."

"Francis, are you speaking of the Egyptian god, Thoth, the one with the head of an ibis bird described by Greek and Roman mystics?"

"Well, er... uh, yes," Francis said, somewhat embarrassed.

"Are you out of your head? Such a thing doesn't exist! Wasn't an emerald amulet of Thoth purported to be the philosopher's stone?" Francis shrugged his shoulders and smiled, still embarrassed. Sarah shook her head, sighed, and continued.

"Francis, that story must be a figment of some ancient sage's imagination, a myth. It can't be real! How can you, an esteemed scholar of antiquity, even hint at such a thing to be true? You are being as silly as those crazy conspiracy theorists who are always writing about chaotic things that happen and blaming them on the Illuminati or some other secret group."

"Well, I'm not sure about conspiracy theories, but some great historical thinkers did not feel that way about the emerald amulets of Thoth. Even the Nubians believed they were real! Now, I am not saying that Thoth had the head of a bird, but...."

"Francis, this is all getting quite surreal. Do you truly believe this could be one of the amulets of Thoth or are you pulling my leg?"

"Well, it just might be one of the Emerald Amulets of Hermes Trismegistus," he said excitedly. "This and the scroll could be what Nostradamus used, along with a translation of *De Mysteriis Egyptorum* prophecies written by Iamblichus, a Neo-Platonist in the fourth century. He might have used them both to write his odd prophecies over 2,000 years later. Without the key, the prophecies would be extremely difficult – if not impossible – to translate correctly! We have seen that fact to be true over the centuries. There have been all sorts of translations of Nostradmaus' prophecies since they were discovered, and quite often they were dichotomous and even antagonistic." He looked a Sarah, who shook her head in disbelief and changed the subject.

"Is it an emerald? Is the stone cut from pure green beryl? It appears to be, but we will need to analyze it before we can be sure. It will only take a few minutes to do the test once we get back to the tent. However, I don't believe in the existence of any emerald amulets of Thoth, or a god with the head of an ibis that writes history. There has to be a more logical explanation!"

"Yes, that is a possibility. Nevertheless, do you know what this could mean? We may have a pre-Nostradamus Nubian scroll written in the fourth century that predated his published book by close to 2,000 years and might contain similar prophecies as those found in his published manuscript. Do you realize that if that is true, the Nostradamus prophecies will be made completely clear? All of his hidden innuendos and obscurities will be unmasked, and we will know *exactly* what the prophecies say! The new manuscript may have similar prophecies found in the scroll as well. Perhaps similar prophecies were even in *De Mysteriis Egyptorum*! It appears there are also some other data in the manuscript, but all of this is going to take a lot of time to properly translate and authenticate. I will need other expert guidance as well. From my cursory investigation, however, it does appear that we may have the authority to tie all of the ancient prophetic writings together.

"This is a remarkable find; it will be the first time in history that man will have complete knowledge of what Nostradamus' prophecies predict. In addition and most importantly, we have an amulet, which is possibly a means to help us decode the true writings of the various prophecies. Whether the gem is actually one of the Emerald Amulets of Hermes Trismegistus is moot; it may have been designed by a Kushite king or one of his religious scribes. Of course, before we translate anything we need to authenticate the writings of the scroll using the green amulet. That should give us a final and accurate interpretation of Nostradamus' prophecies."

"If what you say is true, Francis, why would these pieces be buried out here? The Nubian scroll makes some sense, possibly even the amulet, but there is no way the Nostradamus manuscript fits into the ancient time line in any conceivable way. I believe the manuscript, the scroll, and the amulet have been purposely brought here from some other area and buried. According to the disturbing of the sand, it happened less than a year to six months ago. It is all strange and troubling. I should have listened to my first impression when I dug down and found the amulet. The sand was too soft, signifying it had been disturbed recently, perhaps as early as six months ago. Something is terribly wrong here. We were meant to find these relics and bring them back to the corporation for some reason."

"Yes, it all seems to make sense… the contract with the corporation, the precisely selected site by the Department of Defense, and especially the unwillingness of the corporation to tell us what was of importance to find here."

"That's so true! By the way, you stated that there are other historically authenticated citations concerning an amulet that might have been related to Nostradamus and his odd writings… what are those? This is an area in which I am not properly educated."

"Yes, there are historically authenticated data concerning such an amulet. It was reported by Catholic officials that an amulet was found missing from Nostradamus' neck in the 1700's when his coffin was moved to a wall in a church. Prior to that time, the amulet was reported seen around the neck of his skeleton. The number 1700, some writings, and an image of an ibis were also reported carved or etched on it. The amulet we have found could very well be that same amulet; everything appears to fit. Some different historians stated that inside his coffin was something, I believe they mentioned a scroll, that later went missing. However, since no scroll was reported to have been inside his coffin, I believe it was the amulet, not a scroll, that they meant was the key to the translation of the prophecies. However, now that we have found a scroll, too, it could be that it was this scroll as well as the amulet that was to be used to accurately translate his prophecies."

"You believe it was both the scroll and the amulet that was to be used for the translation of his prophecies."

"Yes, I think that could be true. It makes sense."

"Francis, do you feel that these artifacts were illegally obtained? That could have prevented them from bringing the artifacts out legally, therefore they had to obtain a contract with the Sudanese to bring them out of the country."

"I think that is probably true. I remember something else, too. I read something last year about some artifacts being stolen from the Egyptian Museum in Cairo. I don't remember the article saying anything specifically about what we have here, but they might have purposely kept the identity of the stolen artifacts out of the news." Francis paused, shook his head, and went back to his discourse about the stone. "It was once said by a 13th century historian that if one locates the emerald stone of Thoth and is able to decipher it, a map of the hallways underneath the earth will be opened and all the clues to the future will be revealed."

"Francis, be real! That is definitely a myth about hell."

"Perhaps, but it could have meant some other underground system that has been dug into the earth." Francis paused. "Sarah, I remember being told something by one of my more creative American students at the Sorbonne. He said he once read from some source that the published Nostradamus prophecies outlined what the USA and their foreign allies had planned to do during the latter part of the 20th and first part of the 21st centuries." Francis looked at Sarah, feeling a bit embarrassed again.

"My goodness, Francis, first the emerald translating stone of Thoth and now a conspiracy theory?"

Francis shrugged his shoulders, hoping Sarah wouldn't think him a total nut. He then looked at her and waited for another negative reaction. Sarah sighed but did not laugh.

"Okay, Francis, go ahead and tell me. What did he say about some conspiracy?"

Francis, feeling somewhat relieved, smiled broadly. "The student said, to help destroy any possibility of public retaliation against future severe American federal laws implemented by the White House such as surveillance of US citizens without court warrants, wearing away of the voting rights of minorities, as well as the taking of state national guards for federal service such as wars, purposeful and nefarious lies would be used. You have already observed much of that during the last five presidencies, haven't you?" Sarah frowned and nodded. He continued. "Then the student said that the government, under special circumstances, could illegally use taxpayers' monies for unspecified secret projects and never report their use. Many of these secret projects would be initiated in the Pentagon with what are called black funds. He also talked about the use of torture as a legitimate action by blocking of the habeas corpus writ for enemies caught and kept out of the United States."

Sarah shook her head. "Many of those things have come to pass, Francis, but I can't believe that they were *all* prophesized by Nostradamus!"

"Yes, well… the student also said that the prophecies mentioned something called Executive Order 11490, strengthened by President Nixon. It allows the government to bypass the Constitution and take control of every aspect of the states, which includes the unlimited use of the citizens of the state for any reason under a sanctioned national emergency."

"Well, if such an order exists, thank goodness we have not had the United States declare a national emergency yet!"

"Well, look at what powers your FEMA has during natural emergencies. One of the other things mentioned was that over 130 massive secret underground facilities would be built across America. They would be underground city-bases with the amenities of a modern city. Those facilities were to have been started in the 60's."

"Francis, that last prediction is preposterous! Someone or some group, if huge underground facilities were actually being dug up, would have seen the mountains of dirt taken out from the ground. At least one person would have gotten inside one of the 130 underground base-cities! Someone that had been stationed in one of them would have eventually said something about them, too, don't you think?"

"Yes, I guess so. But then again, perhaps the American people were too busy working and living to believe in conspiracies, look for huge dirt piles, or even bother to worry about one if they did see it." Sarah was looking at him incredulously. "It seems a lot of the Nostradamus prophecies have already been fulfilled, according to some who say they translated the prophecies correctly, but I just don't know. Perhaps it is all a coincidence, or perhaps some conspiracy nuts were just saying that was what was prophesized after it happened. Who really knows for sure!

"Your question about someone finding and not questioning any of the 130 huge underground facilities is an excellent question, though. It does seem totally illogical and preposterous not to have *some* evidence of such facilities after 40-something years! Then again, a lot of things are exposed but get no media attention and therefore they are never looked into! I mean, does the American public really care about underground facilities? If they don't care, the media doesn't bother reporting it."

The two looked at each other as the cool night wind gusting off the Sudan sand marched through their thoughts like an icy phantom. They looked anxiously around the dig and, failing to observe a dark-hooded figure standing in the shadows of the pyramid, continued talking while sitting on a small sandstone boulder. As they continued to discuss the finding, reflected beams from the large desert moon crisscrossed their bodies like ancient bindings.

"Francis, I believe now more than ever that the Nostradamus manuscript, the ancient Nubian scroll, and the amulet were what we were sent here to find! I believe the Department of Defense, someone in the government, or both wanted the Nostradamus prophecies found with the amulet. They wanted the key to translating Nostradamus' cryptic poems, if it is actually the key, so that they would have clues to something that is prophesized to happen. They might even have been the ones who arranged someone to steal the antiquities from the museum. They probably could not take the chance of getting them out of the country illegally. They also did not want, for some reason, any media exposure of what was found. A legal two-country contract to take antiquities out of *this* area from *this* dig was the ideal ruse!"

"I think you are right, Sarah... then someone in the government or the corporation hid them here sometime this past year for us to find and send back to America legitimately!"

"I think that is very likely, Francis. Remember, they were given close to 50 million dollars by the Department of Defense to find something out here, and I don't believe that all of the artifacts out here are worth that amount of money! It definitely has to be something else worth billions, like true prophecies of the future and the key to decoding them."

"My god, do you think the United States Defense Department believes that they could control the destinies of the world?" Francis whispered.

"I don't know, Francis. Perhaps it is not even the government or the Department of Defense but just some people at the highest levels of government. I personally haven't liked the actions of some of the last presidents we elected in regard to clandestine activities. During the 21st century I also can't say we have done too well electing any of our congressmen and senators. However, I can't believe our presidents were personally responsible for a lot of the bad data on which they based their stupid decisions. The problem is that it is impossible to stop radical ideologists from getting into the highest levels of government to influence those at the top." She sighed and changed the subject.

"Francis, we have to hide the amulet, the scroll, and the manuscript until we can positively authenticate them and then decipher the prophecies accurately. If the prophecies contain data that could predict chaos in the world, we will need to tell someone important and trustworthy in a high level of power about it. I have no idea who that might be right now, and don't trust anyone except President Obama himself. But we know we cannot get to him directly!"

"Sarah, we also cannot send the amulet, scroll, or the Nostradamus manuscript to the corporation with the other artifacts found this week. Nor can we put them down in the site log of artifacts found, an act that could not only get us fired but also ruin our reputations and possibly careers."

"Yes, I know. We only have a few months left on the dig; that will give us enough time to hide the relics and figure out how to get them out of here without the others noticing, especially the corporation man. Then we need to plan how to get them someplace away from the corporation once we return home."

Francis shook his head sadly.

"Yes, then we need to find some more trusted experts to help in authenticating the items. Eventually, if we *do* find them to be authentic or perhaps even if we don't, we need to translate and decode the prophecies found in the new Nostradamus manuscript. If it is a fake, it is done for a specific purpose!"

Sarah looked around the area and then glanced at Francis. She put her finger to her lips as she noticed a tall hooded figure with a face of obsidian walking about six yards from the area where they sat.

They were not aware that their entire conversation had been overheard. They had not felt the nearness of the sandal-footed, hooded monk. They would in the future, however, for the hooded man would become an extremely important figure in their lives. In fact, the existence of the hooded figure would play a significant role in life and death as Sarah and Francis would attempt to escape from the clutches of the corporation and black covert CIA agents with the purloined relics.

Sarah and Francis hid the relics in their personal clothes bags, blew out the kerosene lamp, and tried to go to sleep. The sandal-footed hooded figure with the ebony face listened outside their tent and sighed as he looked out at the massive orange moon that kept dark secrets in the night. He then walked about 30 meters from the tent and dialed a number on a satellite cell phone.

"Yes, this is Faisal. The items have been recovered.... Yes, Dr. Addison and Dr. Vachon found them.... No, they have not informed the others and will not. I overheard their conversation. They suspect that the corporation and individuals from the Department of Defense might be in some type of conspiracy.... No, they have no idea concerning the complicity of some people in the White House. They also tied one of the items to those stolen recently from the museum.... Yes, they are very bright people.... Yes, Sire, I will follow them when they leave the area if I cannot get the items back while they are here.... Goodbye."

The hooded man sighed, looked up to the stars, frowned, and disappeared into the darkness. The man at the other end of the conversation looked up at the orange moon drifting across the sky and then went back to his prayers.

Dr. Addison and Dr. Vachon stared at the stars and moon out of the webbed windows in the tent and wondered what the significance of the relics and especially the Nostradamus manuscript really was. They would find out soon that they were all very significant and very dangerous to the lives of countless people, including theirs.

Chapter Three
The Conspirators

Two weeks prior to a perilous incident that would take place at Keller's Knoll, a group of executives from the Archeology Archives Corporation were meeting in an opulent penthouse suite in a steel and glass high rise in downtown San Francisco, California. The room was ostentatiously paneled in expensive, delicate Indonesian pecan wood and the hardwood teak floor was partially covered with an exquisite 12th century Oriental rug. Dark, polished antique mahogany chairs with plush, soft, dark maroon kid-leather seats held angry men dressed in dark gray cashmere suits and silk ties and two women dressed in light gray silk pant suits. They all sat around a long, polished mahogany table. The room reeked of ill-gained opulence and uncontrolled greed.

A large, brusque German with a bald head, prominent nose, and dark, bushy eyebrows spoke fiercely in broken English as his blue eyes flitted angrily from one person to the next around the mahogany table in the ornate room. His small eyes contained darkness as they stared furiously at the group.

"How did Dr. Addison and Dr. Vachon find the Nostradamus manuscript, Nubian scroll, and amulet without detection and smuggle them out of the Sudan area?" He looked at Daniel with a fierce scowl. "Damn it, I thought that you had a security person at the excavation site to watch over Dr. Addison and make sure everything found in the dig was logged in and sent back to us! I am sure our friends in DC didn't spend a half million dollars to hide the artifacts only to have them removed from the site without our knowledge. We know for sure the items were found because two men from the Department of Defense went to the area after our people left and confirmed that the artifacts had been dug up. We have been given no-bid contracts amounting to hundreds of millions of dollars over the years because we were trustworthy and unquestioning. Is there no one able to speak about this travesty?"

Daniel Smyth, the tall, slender head of security, blanched and then answered, "I had a very capable man there, Max! However, he did not see Dr. Addison or Dr. Vachon find the manuscript and scroll, nor the amulet. He has no idea how they hid and removed the items from the area. Dr. Addison and Dr. Vachon had to have been distrustful of him from the beginning. They didn't even show their own team their finds. It was very unfortunate that one of the others on the team or my man did not find the items first. That wasn't possible, of course, since we couldn't lead anyone directly to the relics. That would have been highly questionable. They must have worked after the rest of the team went to camp, hidden their finds immediately, finished their work at night, and told no one. Max, they had to have been suspicious of us at the outset. If I had known, I would have had them watched more closely. They probably worked on the manuscript and scroll at night."

Maximilian glared at Daniel.

"I don't like the idea that they have the manuscript and could have a hint of its significance. Dr. Vachon, as you all know, is an expert in ancient languages. He could have already translated one or more of the prophecies, meaning that he and Dr. Addison could at this very moment know something of significance, which could be detrimental to Mr. William's plan!"

Daniel flinched and said, "They had to have smuggled the items in some of their personal gear. When they got back to headquarters they must have hidden them until they could get them out of the area safely. The incident was unforeseeable."

The German glared at him and yelled, "*Ja, natürlich würden Sie irgendeine dumme Entschuldigung haben, aber Sie sind da verantwortlich!*"

Daniel didn't understand German, but he understood that Maximilian held him responsible for the problem and he needed to find a way out of it.

"We know for sure they were never in any of the other bundles of artifacts," Derek Murray from operations stated. "My people checked everything thoroughly."

Vice President of Procurements Horace Coopman, a

large, obese man with a scar from his right eye to the right side of his chin and an obvious tic, spoke angrily with a Flemish accent.

"We should have gotten rid of those two traitors years ago. Dr. Addison has been a problem ever since the fiasco in Iraq after the antiquities stolen from the museum were found and taken out of her hands without notification. Dr. Addison voiced fierce opposition to the fact that we took them from her possession. She said it was something totally out of compliance with normal protocol.

"They are not the trusted, unquestioning team members we figured they were when we hired them. I put her in her place at a meeting and thought that would be the end of it. I placed her and her team outside of the US on minor digs in various countries for years. I figured if I kept her busy, she would settle down. I thought she had since she did such a good job on the other excavations and never complained about the Iraqi relics again. She voiced the same concern this time when she returned. She said the relics found in Sudan were taken before her team had an opportunity to inspect them.

"If we had known the proper academic protocol, we could have done something to assuage her at the time. However, as I look back on it now, her opposition to us taking the artifacts found in Sudan was not expressed with much force. We, of course, thought that we would find the scroll, manuscript, and amulet among the artifacts that we took before giving them back to be authenticated and cataloged."

"But you didn't!" Max replied angrily.

"I have to believe now, Max, that that her opposition this time was just a ruse to throw us off, and you are correct, we did not find the three artifacts."

"Dr. Addison and Dr. Vachon left one night and didn't return the following day. I am sure they took the manuscript, scroll, and amulet with them at that time. They had to have been suspicious of us the whole time, damn them!" Daniel Smyth stated angrily.

Maximilian looked out the huge plate glass window to the

streets of San Francisco below. People the size of mice moved restlessly back and forth and up and down the cracked cement sidewalks under neon signs with the odors of fast food wafting in their nostrils. The people below looked insignificant, and to those at the meeting, they were.

"What made you believe that they had stolen the items?" Max asked when he turned around.

"One of the security guards and one of the team members saw them working late at night on some manuscript with what appeared to be a green stone just hours before they left. The items were not found in the laboratory. They probably noticed that they were being watched. One person also saw that they were doing something with the computer. They were probably scanning the scroll and the manuscript into it. After that, they probably made a copy for themselves and permanently erased the data. Damn, we should have gotten rid of them years ago." Daniel pounded his fist on the table, causing some of the others to jump.

"No one voiced any serious objections against them before Daniel, including you and Horace. How the hell was I expected to do anything about it?" David Doyle, the director of human resources, answered with a splenetic grating to his voice. He was a tall, thin man with the demeanor of a vulture and almost hissed when he spoke. He glared at Coopman as Smyth turned red and then shook his head crossly as he fidgeted with his fountain pen.

Maximilian Vogel glared at Horace then at David.

"Enough! Let's face it," he bellowed as he looked out at the executives sitting around the table. "Every one of you screwed up! I should have been notified of your concerns many times over the years. Even her diatribes against what we were doing in Iraq went unchallenged by any of you, except for you, Coopman. However, you didn't see it fit to notify me of the altercation after it happened."

"I thought I had handled it, I didn't see any need to bother you on the matter!"

"You all must have heard something about it after it happened! Why was I never told? Then the questioning of our integrity by Dr. Addison went unabated a second time, and again I was not told. No one said anything to me about her and her annoyance over our taking other artifacts during the past years. I would never have sent her to recover the items from the Sudan site if I had been properly informed. The final and most devastating act was their ability to conceal what they found in Sudan and take the items from our supposedly theft-proof building. Where the hell was all of our security during these times? Why didn't we put someone on them 24/7?" he yelled as he glared at Daniel again. He looked back at the rest and said, "Every damn one of you was lax and are equally responsible for *dieses schreckliche Fiasko!* Er, this horrible fiasco. What we have to do now is remedy the problem by finding them, the manuscript, the scroll, and the amulet. Daniel, get your best people on it. I want the relics back immediately and I don't want to ever see those two scientists again! Do you understand?"

"Yes, I'll put Omar Awad on it immediately!"

Director of Operations Derek Murray, an overweight black man of about 50, put his $38.00 Cuban cigar in an ashtray and spoke in a deep, raspy voice.

"Our operational paradigm is in peril unless we get the items back, Max. The corporation could lose billions of dollars from the government in the future and that doesn't include the expensive relics that we confiscated for ourselves. The manuscript and the amulet, which is the key to decoding the prophecies according to Darren Williams, was our free pass to untold billions. Daniel, I hope that the people you send this time are a hell of a lot better than the last two! You had better pray they are!"

Daniel turned ashen.

"Omar is my best man and I will send a team of two others with him for backup. Dr. Addison and Dr. Vachon will not be a bother to us much longer!"

Maximilian glanced over at a beautiful, tall woman with a face of ebony stone who had been silent throughout the meeting.

"Mary is there to spin the problem if we don't locate the

relics and someone starts digging for information. The Iraqi relics and the hundreds of other antiquities we have kept for ourselves or sold on the black market for millions could also be a problem."

Director of Public Relations Mary Drew, a statuesque black woman, nodded her head.

"Those things are all definitely a serious problem for us and there is no way in the world that we can spin that type of damaging evidence away. We are all toast if that information gets out. We can't blame Dr. Addison and Dr. Vachon for all of it, either, since they are our employees. Blaming the government for allowing us to do what we have done would never be accepted, either. The people in the White House would spin it so that it was all our doing and all of us would end up in prison. We can't even say that we were given the no-bid contracts and gave part of the money back. You remember, there were no written contracts for that part of the process. Once it gets out that we have dealt illegally with stolen artifacts, there could also be a Senate investigation into the rest of our activities, such as those concerning the Iraqi museum relics, many of which never got back to the museum!"

Maximilian looked at the glass case containing the priceless Iraqi artifact and nodded. He looked at Mary, who he had personally hired six months before primarily to satisfy the government that the corporation had a racially integrated female executive workforce. He wondered inwardly how such a beautiful face as hers could contain such a stolid, careworn look. It seemed she lived in a world of frozen bitterness, obedient to some inner icy will. He wondered what made the woman tick. He had no trouble figuring out his other executives; they were all just materialistic and greedy bastards like him who would do anything to amass wealth. Mary was unique and disturbing as well; there was something mysterious about her and it bothered him. He often wondered what had happened to his last PR woman. She had simply disappeared without a word and was never found.

Vice President of Technical Support Johanna Klimas sighed heavily then spoke.

"We need to develop a plan to destroy all of our computer data as well as financial and technical data within minutes if these things start to come out. If worse comes to worse, we also need a plan to get our money out of the corporation account to offshore banks and escape from America. If the authorities and the public find out we have stolen antiquities from other countries under government contracts, it will be all over for us. It could also be all over for your government friends. They have been able to spin a lot of things in the past, but it might be difficult to spin something as disastrous as this."

"I have some taped phone conversations of Darren Williams concerning many of our mutual illicit activities, including the Iraqi incident. He has no knowledge he was taped," Maximilian stated. "That might help down the road."

Johanna shook her head. "No good, Max… that would never stand up in court, and out of court it would simply be our word against theirs. They could say that the tape was fake and make us look like fools or a bunch of crooked frauds."

Johanna was 50 years old, fragile-haired, and tediously featured. She was a very sober woman and was always taken seriously. This time was no exception. The people sitting at the table shifted uncomfortably in their seats and most shuddered at the thought of losing their wealth, leaving their positions of status and influence, and giving up their multimillion-dollar homes and possibly even their families. To some, the latter problem was the least of their worries. They figured they would at least keep their fortunes intact if they were able to flee before a Congressional investigation was initiated and their passports were taken. If worse came to worse, they might be able to escape to another country with no extradition, and then they would be safe.

Maximilian nodded his large head and grimaced.

"Yes, you are correct. Johanna, develop a plan immediately and find a way to offshore our assets to new accounts so that no one can get to them, especially our friends in DC with their far-reaching tentacles. The rest of you think about a solution to the problem. We will meet again as soon as Francis and Sarah are located and erased, or if the worst scenario occurs!

Now all of you, *nichts wie raus hier*! Er, get the hell out of here!"

The German of dark wealth pondered the curse that hid within his mind. A brutal blackness expanded as it fell upon the office like a pall of bitter prophecies. He sat coldly brooding in the empty office. He was aware that his greed and especially his antipathy of Arabs and Jews alike might have abetted bringing the present situation to fore. He could have tiptoed around and not accepted the latest contract when his contact told him about the Nubian scroll, the Nostradamus manuscript, and the amulet. He was also told that one of the prophecies dealt with the mutual annihilation of the two factions of his disdain with new, recently developed super bombs and he was hooked.

His major aim in life had always been the amassing of extreme wealth, unconstrained power, and unhindered influence at the highest levels, but his desire to destroy both the Arabs and the Jews was important as well. Detonating small atomic bombs in the Middle East and Israel would not have bothered him.

Information which would seal his fate was now in the unaware hands of Dr. Addison and Dr. Vachon. He grunted and thought to himself that they might be able to determine that he was in accord with what the high-ranking government officials wanted when they first contacted him in regard to the prophecies. However, that was untrue; he didn't have much information on the use of the relics, and he didn't care at first. He exhaled noisily and picked up a gold phone. Up to this point, he had been thoroughly safe on his upward road to riches. He was now worried. He dialed an unlisted number in Washington DC.

∞

"Yes, this is Maximilian Vogel. I need to speak with the president's personal counsel, Darren Williams, immediately…. Yes, it is extremely urgent…. Yes, I said *extremely* urgent!"

After Maximilian's phone call, three men in Washington DC were heatedly discussing the problem of the missing scroll, manuscript, and amulet. Since the president was in Asia and the vice president was in Pakistan trying to assuage their leaders that

America still stood by them, the meeting was held surreptitiously in the Oval Office. Darren Williams secretly coveted the Oval Office, but he knew he could never *buy* it, even with his tens of billions of dollars. The skeletons in his closet were too numerous and too pernicious to escape public scrutiny no matter how elaborate the spin to hide them.

Darren looked around the room from behind the president's huge desk.

"Gentlemen, our perfect scheme and our future wealth and power are now threatened. We can't delay. Precise measures must be put into play immediately. The Nubian scroll, the amulet key, and the Nostradamus manuscript that were to be sent to us from the Archeology Archives Corporation are missing."

A collective gasp was heard around the table.

"When we stole the Nubian scroll and had the Nostradamus manuscript written to match the first few prophecies, we had a flawless plan. The green emerald amulet was a stroke of genius. Where was it ever found? Well, no matter. The scroll, being legitimate, could be shown to other experts and then our experts could authenticate the other two items with authority. Since the manuscript appears to be real and the emerald stone looks authentic – and maybe it is – tying them to the Nubian scroll would be a simple process. We could air the find to the public and then use the prophecies against our enemies with our allies.

"It cost us two million dollars to have the damn manuscript forged and another million to have the amulet and scroll stolen and hidden in the sands of Sudan. Extreme care must be exercised in locating those who are thwarting our plan and no tolerance will be shown toward any who try to prevent our scheme from occurring. Even if we have to kill the whole damn lot, we must have those prophecies!" The tall, gray-haired man then hissed in anger. "Remember, '*Novus Ordo Saccularum.*'"

Ralph Anderson of the procurement department and Jon Pierce, special counsel to the vice president, nodded their heads in agreement.

"Jon, the call from Max did not make me feel

comfortable. I have thought about it and I believe we need some covert agents with technical know-how to assure that we get the items back. We already know that the corporation's agents don't have the background to do it. I also don't trust Maximilian and his little greedy gang of parasites at this point. I figure if they find the artifacts, they might take them out of the country themselves and try to sell them. That could lead to the exposure of the manuscript being a forgery. We cannot allow that to happen. All those who know about the manuscript must be eliminated as soon as possible!"

Ralph and Jon fidgeted uncomfortably in their chairs and shook their heads. They were getting uncomfortable with what Darren was saying. He continued. "Jon, you need to discuss the problem with the director of homeland security and get some top CIA agents to assist us in getting the job done. Just be sure you do not make them aware of the real purpose of the request. Tell them it is a top secret national security emergency."

Jon Pierce was a severe-looking man who oozed ex-military and had short brown hair, a narrow face, and deep-set, piercing dark gray eyes. He nodded.

"I'll get on it immediately, Darren."

Darren nodded his head.

"I want only the most covert arm of the CIA on this job, okay, Jon? We need to make sure our part in the Nostradamus scheme is never revealed. I especially want Dr. Addison and Dr. Vachon, the ones who stole the items, found and taken care of permanently. They cannot be allowed enough time to inspect the items and determine their authenticity, nor live to tell their rendition of the story if they have already translated some of the manuscript.

"Once our agents find the Nostradamus manuscript and amulet, have them bring them back here before the corporation agents can get to them. I also want you to get some regular CIA agents to stay as close to all of the executives at the corporation as possible. Have them report to you about what the executives are doing. We may need to take care of them as well! We also need immediate communication if something odd starts to take place at the corporation."

"What about Maximilian's security agents? They are already on the job."

"Yes, I know. Jon, have the CIA agents locate and follow them, which should not be too difficult. Make sure the corporation's security agents don't get to Dr. Addison and Dr. Vachon first. Tell the CIA agents this is a top-secret national security assignment from the highest authority, and they are to tell no one! Tell them that they need to report only to you two and make sure that they know that they must follow *all* instructions immediately and without question. That includes eliminating the corporation agents as well as Dr. Addison and Dr. Vachon, and anyone else that gets in the way. Alert them that the safety of the nation is at risk, which we will try to make happen when we get the items back." He laughed, trying to be upbeat about the dire situation before he continued.

"Jon, I must iterate again, make sure you inform the agents that all directives can only come from either you or Ralph and no one in homeland security, the CIA, FBI, Department of Defense, or any other agency." He stopped for a moment, looked out the window, and turned back to the two men. "As of now, I think the only damaging information involves the corporation itself, not us. However, Max and some of the other executives might have some data implicating us, and of course, we gave them the no-bid contracts in the first place. That is why I want the matter taken care of immediately. Think of a way to spin the story if information is aired to the public, Ralph, and especially if the Nostradamus manuscript is determined to be a forgery. I believe it may be possible that we can blame the executives of the corporation and escape scrutiny since they are nothing but greedy bastards, anyway!"

Darren hesitated, took a sip of his 38-year-old Duncan Taylor blended malt whiskey, nodded, and looked at the two men with a crooked smile before going into his pep talk.

"Gentlemen, since our inception into the highest levels of government, private companies in America like Haliharten, Darkwater, and the Archeology Archives Corporation have been the recipients of millions, even billions, of no-bid contract dollars from the government with hundreds of millions coming back to us. With the Nostradamus manuscript in force, those millions will look like chump change."

Jon then said, "Because of our Iraq and Afghanistan wars, which cost the uninformed and naive taxpayer about $4 trillion as of today, and the tax break for us, which cost the treasury almost a trillion dollars, the USA debt now approaches over $17 trillion. Through Wall Street, we have created pseudo economic wellbeing and then economic disaster simply by causing chaos in various parts of the Middle East by altering interest rates and types of derivative loans. We have been instrumental in raising the cost of crude oil and gasoline at the pump, but we need more chaos to fulfill our monetary needs!"

"That is true, Jon, we always need a new crisis, like a war in Iran, to accomplish real wealth. The bigger the crisis, the more money will land in our hands. Perhaps we can cause some unrest in other Arabian countries, although the Arab spring has created tremendous chaos in many Middle Eastern nations. Just look at the recent housing problems, too… if we can maneuver a bailout like our last banking scheme from the new president, we will make more billions after we get bank regulations removed again. It was brilliant to get the banks to give low interest loans to people who couldn't actually qualify for them, charge initial high fees, increase the interest after a few years, and then sell the loans as being AAA. The bust was totally predictable."

Jon nodded and said, "If we can convince the government that the Nostradamus prophecies are real by using the amulet key and Nubian scroll, we can increase chaos in the public by airing what has been foretold by the new prophecies for the Middle East and Israel as well as for Iran and all the other rich oil-producing nations. We will drop the Department of Defense's new super bombs that we have hidden in one of our underground FEMA bases. We can cause total chaos by dropping them on specific Arab countries. Our conservative Pentagon generals can direct all these activities.

"Then we will blame each bombing on each nation's

neighbor and Israel, as foretold by the Nostradamus prophecies. That will enable us to move in and take over the oil industry in all of the Middle Eastern nations as they mutually annihilate each other. In the end, we will own most of these countries and their oil. We can cut down on dissent by annihilating most of their populations."

Williams shook his head, smiled, and said, "At the same time, because of the bombings, the government will be in a panic and the president will have to declare a national emergency. That will allow us total control over every state and its citizens."

"Darren, are you sure that the government and the public will swallow the authenticity of the Nostradamus prophecies?" Jon asked.

"Well, it appears that patterns were the clues to Nostradamus' predictions. His ability to visualize patterns in other ancient texts and realize their meaning in the future was his genius. The people of his time, and even centuries after, believed his prophecies. We re-designed and altered the manuscript utilizing those identical, unique patterns. It is such a professional modification that the experts would be at least confounded enough about the validity of the manuscript to cause most to accept it, especially with the aid of the scroll, which *is* authentic, and the amulet, which is the key."

"Do you think the academics in the field of languages and primitive history will swallow the emerald stone of Thoth myth?"

"They might, Ralph, why not? A lot of people in the red states still believe that Hussein had weapons of mass destruction, and 60% of our Republican party still supports the war in Afghanistan and would probably support a new war with Iran and North Korea. The ancient antipathy between Shiites and Sunnis, or tribal units such as the Taliban and al Qaeda, or even the terrorist groups in Pakistan against America is legendary and will not go away no matter what is done in those countries. These groups will always hinder any outside military advantage or political unity in the end. This is all lost on a public that is constantly told we must have a victory by whoever is in the White House and held in fear by conservative talking heads and the conservative base. The Sunni-Shia political stalemate and concomitant hatred will exist for the next 1,000 years, regardless of what anyone does. Look at Iraq now… the two sides are still murdering each other." Darren paused momentarily.

"Anyway, to get back to our problem, we will state to the press that the manuscript without the amulet was a conundrum. The preliminary information about the prophecies, when the manuscript is found and translated, could be said to have been at best of nebulous authority. However, the amulet combined with the authentic Nubian scroll proves that the new Nostradamus manuscript is real and therefore the prophecies are true. Our plan, based on what his writings prophesize for our times, will convince others in America and other nations to follow our lead. That will give us our greatest crisis since World War II. We cannot allow the thwarting of our plan by people who have a stupid moral conscience… it could cost us trillions of dollars a year in profit and we could lose our anticipated control of America."

The two men nodded their heads and left the Oval Office, talking quietly. Jon and Ralph had been acquaintances in college, and throughout their time in the White House, their families met at certain gala affairs. Their children were in college together, although they were not intimate friends.

Ralph looked at Jon and shook his head.

"We have a big problem and there is no way we will get any help from Darren if things go sour; it will be every man for himself. We need to protect ourselves, which means we need to consider thwarting the plan itself."

"I was thinking the same thing about our protecting ourselves, Ralph… we need to develop a plan to get out of the country with our families and our wealth if that happens. I don't know about scuttling the plan, though. It might still work and we could end up with tremendous wealth as well as control over the wealth of many other countries. We need to keep close on this, Ralph!"

"Why the hell did we ever get mixed up in Darren's crazy plan, anyway?"

"Well, I for one figured it was nothing more than an innocuous, hair-brained idea in the beginning when he said he found a down-on-his-luck professional forger who could write Nostradamus prophecies perfectly. I mean, who would ever believe in Nostradamus' predictions nowadays anyway? Such a notion seemed ludicrous. I supported getting mixed up in the no-bid contracts, kickbacks from the corporation, and the scheme involving the stolen Iraqi artifacts because it would lead to easy money. Those were simple schemes and we did make a bundle on them. Of course, the ultimate nail in the coffin was when he had the Nubian scroll and amulet stolen from the Egyptian museum and then actually had the Nostradamus manuscript written. Ralph, what about the amulet? Where in the hell did they find that thing?"

"I don't have any idea, but I do know that it is a real emerald."

"At any rate, by the time we were aware of his new plot we were in too deep with his other schemes to *not* go along. Do you really believe that Nostradamus' prophecies for this age would be believed by the public and the rest of the government?"

"Jon, I don't have a clue… but I do know that if all of this starts to come down around us, it will be you and me that are hung." Ralph shook his head and said, "I don't want to be blamed for it and I am sure that is exactly what Darren has in mind if things go wrong. Damn, what do we do now?"

"Well, I think we have to go along with the scheme for now," Jon said as he sighed heavily. "We will decide what to do once the items have been retrieved. I do have access to some covert agents from the outside at this point, but I haven't determined how to use them yet. I don't like having to assassinate innocents, though."

"Yes, we must figure a way out of that!" Ralph stated.

While Jon and Ralph spoke outside, Darren sat down in the president's chair, stared out the window, and thought about what he would have to do if the plan went awry. He was a materialistic man with few moral values and the amassing of wealth and power over others took precedence over everything else in his life. He knew he needed to develop a plan to blame the Archeological Archives Corporation as well as Jon and Ralph, then escape with his wealth if things went awry. He spoke aloud to the heavy air in the empty office.

"The archangel sword of conflagration is in my grasp and all of the world will genuflect at my feet! Even the pope's influence will pale in the light of my awesome authority."

∞

A short time later, a man made a whispered phone call from an office.

"Yes, it's me. Maximilian Vogel just called Darren. Sarah and Dr. Vachon escaped from the corporation headquarters with the items and the corporation have sent some of their security personnel after them to assassinate them."

"Oh my god, do they know where they went?"

"Not yet, but Jon is going to discuss the problem with the director of homeland security. Darren wants some black-funded covert CIA agents to track the two down as well and they are not to be left alive."

"That is terrible news. I will see what Don can find out about that. Are you still safe?"

"I think so, David. There has been nothing to point any fingers me, at least not so far."

"Did Darren ever confide exactly what he had written in the Nostradamus prophecies?"

"Only in general terms; he never gave any full description, just those things which I have already relayed to you. He has kept the rest to himself. I can't see how he could have done this all by himself, though… the man is just not that bright. He also appears to be a little off, if you know what I mean. We know the corporation's role; they are just greedy, materialistic bastards, but I have no idea if even *they* know what the real scheme is all about. I figure none of them really care as long as they get their millions. The mastermind couldn't be one of them; it takes brains for such a scheme and they don't seem to have many. Some other high level person in some other organization has to be involved and we need to find out who."

"Yes, I agree. We have no idea here who that might be, either, but we are working on it. Darren hasn't made any contact with anyone of that ilk, so it has to be face-to-face meetings or the communications are written and put in safe drops."

"Yes, that would be a good assumption. I have to go soon, I have a meeting with the secretary of defense in 20 minutes."

"Does he have a clue that black Pentagon funds have been allocated for the scheme?"

"No, Darren went directly through someone in homeland security. He was given the use some of the trillions of dollars in the Department of Defense's Black Budget fund under a secret provision."

"Perhaps it is a group at the top of Homeland Security or the Pentagon. We have a lot of multi-billionaire brains in that group!"

"Yes, David, that could be it, possibly a new Illuminati group."

"My god, are you still reading those conspiracy novels?" he laughed.

"Well, they do seem to work with the same type of data and espouse the same ideals," he said as he turned a bit pink. He was glad to be on the phone instead of in person.

Chapter Four
Keller's Knoll

The day after returning to the headquarters building from Sudan, Sarah and Francis hid the stolen relics in a sack and placed them under bales of hemp in a supply closet next to their laboratory.

A day later, in the darkness of night when most people had left, Sarah and Francis met in their laboratory.

"Sarah, we need to copy the contents of the manuscript and the scroll into the computer and make a copy," Francis said nervously as he looked around.

It was close to midnight and they only had to contend with security guards who might look into the lab to see what they were doing. They figured that, since they worked late at night quite often, it would not be a problem. Sarah heard a noise in the hallway just as the last of the documents were copied onto a disc. She pushed an icon and permanently erased the data from the computer. She then placed a corrosive virus in the hard drive so that the entire system would be useless and put the disc in her purse.

"It's time we left, Francis. We can't afford to get caught with the artifacts; it could be disastrous."

Little did she realize at the time just *how* disastrous it was going to be. She and Francis put the relics in a case, shut out the light, and headed toward the entrance. When they were halfway there, they heard guards coming up the hall. They immediately ducked into a doorway and waited.

"Where did you see them?" a second guard asked the one who had seen Sarah and Francis in the laboratory.

"They were in the laboratory. It looked like they had a large scroll and a green stone. I think they were scanning something into the computer. I didn't think anything of it until you asked me about them."

After the two guards ran past the room in which Sarah and Francis were hiding, they opened another door and started running down the hall to the laboratory. Sarah and Francis were, at the same time, running to the entrance of the building. The front door was locked, but Sarah had taken a master key and had it duplicated. She used it to unlock the door. The two ran across the parking lot and got in Sarah's car without the security guards seeing them, and within minutes, they had escaped from the corporation. They hid out for the rest of the night in a Motel 6 on the outskirts of San Francisco. Sarah made a call to her sister, Adele, to see if she knew of a place to go.

∞

A few days after leaving San Francisco, Sarah and Francis arrived at Clearlake Oaks, a tiny, picturesque resort town near the shore of Clearlake. It was about 130 miles north of San Francisco. They had hidden Sarah's car in a rented garage in Clearlake and took a cab to their location. They were let out of the cab after the narrow, rutted country road ended in a turnaround. A small, weathered sign that said Keller's Knoll, Woodland Trail, and cabins A, B, C, and D pointed to a wide path covered with deep brown pine needles and small cones from the large pine trees that towered over them. They started walking up a footpath covered with golden pine needles and beautiful, deep blue feathers from blue jays, heading to the top of a mountain where a place called Keller's Knoll was located.

Francis thought it strange that a knoll was on top of a mountain, but didn't mention it since American vernacular was somewhat strange to him. Francis carried the disc with all of the data from the manuscript in a leather carrier he had purchased at the hardware store in town. Along with a few changes of clothes, flashlights, and the relics, the only other thing they had with them was a dark feeling of dread.

"Are you sure this is the place, Sarah?" Francis asked with frustration and a bit of apprehension as he loosened his tie. "It seems awfully remote. It seem the only things up here are enormous trees, bushes, huge rocks, and probably dangerous animals."

"Yes, Francis, this is the way, and don't worry about the

bears or cougars, they don't go after most humans. I hope they don't get excited if they smell a Frenchman!" she chuckled, finally feeling they were in a safe setting.

Dr. Vachon saw no humor in that remark and looked around the area nervously.

"Why are we way up here in this place, anyway?"

"When I called my sister, Ted Barron answered the phone; he's a good friend of my brother, David. I gathered that he and my sister have been dating again. I guess I sounded so frantic that he wanted to know what was wrong. I told him I had a serious problem and needed to find a safe place to stay for a short time where no one could find me. He said his uncle had a cabin up in Clearlake Oaks and I could stay there. He was so nice; he didn't ask for a reason, and of course, I didn't offer one. He said the refrigerator was always stocked with food and there were cords of wood for the fireplace under the porch. I plotted the direction to the cabin on a map and that was that. I told him to tell Adele that I had called her and would try to contact her later. Anyway, the place sounds great for now."

Unfortunately, the corporation had tapped and monitored the sister's phone conversations after Sarah had fled the headquarters and overheard the conversation with Ted about the cabin. Their personnel drove immediately toward Clearlake Oaks, followed – unbeknownst to them – by two covert CIA agents.

Sarah looked at Francis when he had inquired about the safety of the cabin and asked, "Do you anticipate any problems?"

Francis thought for a minute, shrugged his shoulders, and then looked at his cell phone, frowning as he noticed that it was out of range and he had no chance of using it.

"Except for us having no communication, I guess not. We should have purchased satellite phones before coming up here to the middle of nowhere." He paused, looking ahead. "Since you have the map, there's a fork in the road. One trail leads to the north and the other to the south; which trail do we take?"

"Good question... let's see." She laid out the map and oriented it. "Okay, it's the one to the left between those two huge pine trees."

The sun was setting. The verdant mountains turned dull pink in the west, and on the east horizon far below the mountain, there was only a hint of pink and orange daylight. The two took the fork in the road and started up a narrow trail. The falling sun continued painting the huge cumulus clouds dark orange and fiery red, fading into a dusty pink and eventually a soft pinkish white against a dark blue sky. The scientists followed the needle-covered trail through mammoth pine trees that reached up to the sky. They passed dark green junipers as they edged through tall, skinny jack pines. They bypassed dark red-barked manzanita trees that stuck out onto the trail, all with the help of their small flashlight.

All of a sudden, they heard a crash of brush and saw a large, dark shape moving stealthily to their left.

"What the hell is that?" Francis asked, pointing the flashlight in the direction of the din and feeling more uncomfortable than before.

"I don't know, Francis, no one knows where we are… it couldn't be a person."

"Oh, great! That really makes me feel better about what it is, since I know what it *isn't*!" He moved closer to Sarah nervously.

Unfortunately, she did not know that corporation security personnel, followed by CIA agents, were also heading toward the cabin located on Keller's Knoll. The noise in the bushes soon abated and they continued on the trail for about a quarter of a mile followed by the lurking shadow. The sun dipped behind the hills below and cast the area in a starlit, muted darkness. They looked around nervously and walked carefully with the small ray of light pointing at the path.

They heard the noise again just as they approached a cabin, but upon looking around, saw nothing. Francis nervously beamed his flashlight on the structure. He could see that the cabin had been there for years through seasons of rain and snow. It had a dilapidated roof for birds and God to peek through in various spots, day and night. Francis looked askance and sighed. Sarah smiled as if she was held aloof from the ghastly sight by some charmed right. A sign in front said Barron's Basilica cabin B. Ted's uncle was a Catholic and a wry humorist, but not much of a roofer or fixer-upper.

The cabin was a rustic faded green with tall, thin jack pines flanking the sides. Sarah went up to the door, reached above the frame, and found the key where Ted said it would be. She put it in the lock and, with some struggle, opened the door. As the two went inside, the female puma watched for a moment from behind some bushes then headed toward its den and cubs further up the trail. She felt safe now that the humans were gone.

The cabin was cold, but unlike the outside, it was inviting and had an innocent and safe feeling to it. There was a large natural creek stone fireplace located to the south between two tall windows, and a large pewter crucifix molded and cemented into a polished stone of white quartz in the center. The room contained several old mohair sofas, three well-used brown leather chairs, and sundry tables, most with books on them. The hallway across from the living room went to two bedrooms and another smaller room that Ted's uncle appeared to have used as his study. The kitchen-dining room was small, yet cozy and handy. The cupboards were full of food, as were a freezer and the large 20-year-old refrigerator.

Francis took his gear to one of the bedrooms and plopped on the bed, musing over the situation as he took off his suit jacket. He mumbled to the knotty walls.

"Does Sarah not know my soul to be less vigorous than hers, with a refined need for music and gaiety of the metropolitan scene and not the wild, feral noises of the forest? I am not made for running and hiding, traversing dusty forest paths or blistering and thirsty dunes of hardened sand, which lay fallow as they hide white bones. I am but a simple theoretical professor who longs for the safety and smells of his old, moldy laboratory and the melodic sounds of the bustle of a Parisian city. Why did I ever assume I should be involved in excavations to round out my life?" In a short time, he was fast asleep, still dressed.

Sarah was too antsy to sleep and instead laid out the

manuscript and the amulet and attempted to start decoding the multi-language verses. She had only a slight hint of success and finally gave up and turned on the teapot. She fixed herself some toast and sat looking out the windows into the darkness speckled with sparkling stars as she sipped her dark tea. She heard a wolf in the distance, shuddered, and wrapped her arms around herself, remembering a stanza of a poem called *The Second Coming* by Yeats.

"'Turning and turning in the widening gyre; The falcon cannot hear the falconer; Things fall apart; the centre cannot hold; Mere anarchy is loosed upon the world, the blood-dimmed tide is loosed, and everywhere the best lack all conviction, while the worst are full of passionate intensity.'" After quoting the passage, she pulled off her boots, got undressed, and slid under the welcoming sheets.

A noise awakened Francis and he saw the faint glint of something high above their cabin. He grabbed a pair of night vision binoculars and saw a man with a pair of binoculars peering at the cabin, which was partially hidden in a heavy mist that grew murkier with each moment.

"Sarah, we have to get out of here! Someone has found us!"

"Oh my god, how could they? How could anyone know we were up here?" she said nervously. "We'll have to run for it. Out the back door, Francis!"

They grabbed their gear and the artifacts and ran out the back door to a wide trail that meandered down the mountain, eventually reaching the small resort city over a mile below. They ran across the moonlit meadow behind the cabin, knee-deep in dead blooms, remnants of once vibrant flowers. The persisting tall grass, a dusty pale yellow, serving as feed for lambs and sheep and wandering deer, made an obvious path that could be seen and followed easily as they ran through it and tramped it flat.

About 25 minutes after Sarah and Francis had run out of the cabin, the two corporation security agents reached it. They went inside but found no one there. Omar Awad cursed and, after looking around the cabin, holstered his gun. He and one of his agents, Irina Kotov, stepped outside to use their night vision binoculars to look down the mountain at the trail that wandered to the small resort town far below. They saw the crushed yellow grass trail to the rear of the cabin and figured Sarah and Francis had made it. They couldn't see anything beyond the meadow, though, since the trail was obscured due to the heavy brush and trees as well as the darkness. A dark gray, dense fog covered the north side of the mountain. Omar picked up his satellite phone and called his other agent who, before Sarah and Francis had fled, had hiked on another trail far from the cabin to lower ground, about 1,000 meters or so from the top of Keller's Knoll.

"Yide, they are not here. Have you seen them down there?"

"No, are you sure they were there at all?"

"Daniel Smyth said they should be in this cabin. He said he overheard a conversation on a tapped phone. Sarah was talking to someone named Ted. There is also evidence that someone has been in the cabin recently, so they should be around here someplace."

Sarah and Francis, after racing out the back door and across the meadow, had started sprinting down the trail that was slowly being stifled in a heavy mist as they got closer to town. The moon was almost invisible. Sarah, being the faster runner, was in front. They continued running until they passed the vicinity of another cabin, this one labeled cabin C. As Francis turned a corner a few hundred yards from the cabin, his foot slipped on a rock hidden in a pile of leaves and he fell, twisting his ankle. He yelled, so Sarah stopped and ran back to him. The dawn was just starting to break up the darkness a bit.

"Oh my god, Francis! What happened? Can you walk?"

"I don't think so, Sarah.... I tripped on a rock in the stupid leaves and banged up my ankle. It's either broken or twisted... I can't walk on it. You'll have to run ahead. Pull me over to that pile of leaves off the trail and cover me up. You can come back and get me later after you think things are safe."

"I can't do that, Francis! I can't leave you here!"

"You have to or we will both be lost! Here, take the disc, too."

After finally agreeing and placing leaves over Francis to hide him, Sarah took the disc out of the leather pouch and put it in her satchel along with the manuscript and amulet, then set out running again. Behind her was a hooded figure running down the trail where she had just been about 10 minutes before. The figure stopped for a moment and walked over to where a pile of leaves covered Francis. He saw Francis' eyes looking at him in fear. He gave Francis a long stare, then a perceptive nod and continued running after Sarah. Omar and his agents were now in pursuit as well after briefly spotting the two with their night binoculars about 10 minutes before.

Yide was waiting far below the cabin with his gun in hand to seize Sarah and Francis when they rounded the corner on the trail that ran alongside a steep cliff. Sarah saw a glint from something metallic far below as she rounded a corner. She left the wide trail she was on and veered off on a narrow deer path trailing off to the east. She was able to see better now.

The sun was just starting to come up over the mountains to the east. The hooded figure between Omar, Irina, and Dr. Addison noticed her dark outline in the distance. A heavy gray mist covered the area, but he was able to see her go off the main trail. When he reached the area, he saw the narrow deer path and followed it. The darkening fog slowed the pair's progress as they proceeded cautiously down the small craggy path that was carved in many places into the side of steep shale cliffs. It was as if they were in a murky dream and drifting slowly into an abyss. Omar and Irina went past the deer trail where Sarah and the hooded man had left the main trail and, 10 minutes later, rounded the corner where Yide was waiting.

"Yide, what the hell is happening? Where is Dr. Addison?" Omar yelled in bewildered shock.

Yide nodded his head as he lowered his gun.

"She didn't come this way, Omar... I don't know where she is!"

Omar leaned against the mountainside and gazed angrily

down the steep cliff into a murky nothingness. He could not see anything clearly on the trail due to the heavy fog that covered the valley below. His mind went back to his beginnings and he whispered, partially to himself and partially to the haze below.

"I am forceful and cunning, but my experienced hands are empty with no fair prey. Did she feel the vibrations of my dark soul and escape because of it? In the dusky mist and distance below she runs free, but her eyes are still fit for tears and the nightmares I will bring her!"

"What did you say, Omar?" Irina asked as she looked at his angry, contorted face and demented eyes. She had noticed a definite change in Omar's behavior during the past 15 hours and it scared her.

He answered harshly.

"Nothing of importance to you, Irina. Yide, follow the trail back to the cabin. Perhaps they went back on another trail. Irina, you and I will follow the trail to the town."

In the subtle wretchedness of the foggy morning clothed in semi-darkness, the indistinct image of a hooded man materialized amid misty shadows on the wooded path above the small northern village of Clearlake Oaks. He paused in silence, motionless, and watched intently with mysterious intentions. Above, the dull reflection of the morning sun gleamed through the mist like a muted Chinese lantern made of rice paper. The tip of the orange orb began to slowly rise over pewter mountains in a slow, seemingly motionless effort. The dark umbra started carefully down the treacherous, narrow lane that slithered into dense fog, following the frantic jogging figure below. White churchyard steeples glimmered in the dull sunbeams of the emerging morn, clothing the countryside in a misty yellow tint with scarce a dream of sound except the crushing of leaves by small feet madly striding.

Sarah continued in a frenzied haste toward a holy church standing dizzy and vague with white spires reaching upward to the obscure heavens. The steeples were coiled on buoyant fingers of mist. She stopped and, gasping for air from dread and exertion, stood anxiously among dew-covered blades of grass. She turned quickly at a noise in the distance and stared fearfully back at the footpath dressed in murkiness. She heard the dull thud of oncoming feet and scurried ahead to join a stirring group of elderly people emerging from an early morning mass.

Figures silent and devout, transfigured by the flame of the morning sun that bathed the earth with renewed spirit, stood quietly talking in hushed, pious voices. She hesitated and then escaped into the midst of the devout crowd, restless and afraid. The sun fully emerged, bathing the crowd in the golden rays of a gentle dawn. A temperate image of a priest in a black robe stood quietly by huge, gaping carved oak doors that opened from a shadowy, ancient solitude out into the scarlet-hued new day.

Sarah sighed as she observed the enchanting stained glass windows brimming with golden fingers of light on each side of the priest. He was swathed in a circle of yellow light. He caught her staring at him, then with faint hesitancy, looked at her and smiled. She sighed and, in the wavering space of finite time, smiled back.

The priest was an average-looking, somewhat stout middle-aged man with a round, cheerful face, joyful eyes of light blue, and wisps of tussled graying hair falling carelessly down across his brow, now wrinkled in close observation.

The apparition, revealed in the illumination of the sun, stopped abruptly. He watched as Sarah fled into the emerging crowd. He pulled the black hood further over his ebony face after seeing a priest standing by a huge yawning door and glancing his way. An impulse, sudden and intense, subdued into a quiet stillness as the umbra moved stealthily around the corner of the church into the hushed shadows of the subsiding mist and disappeared. The priest watched the form as it retreated into the murkiness of the fog. His face was puzzled and his brow wrinkled as he glanced over to the young woman who now stood a few feet from him, also watching the mysterious figure vanish, and wearing a mask of dark dread. He saw that she was in terror of the person. He frowned as he watched the hooded individual proceeded further into the darkness.

Sarah looked back at the father, walked up to him, and

whispered hoarsely and quietly, "Father, I have eluded my dark captor in the dawn's reflection. What am I to do now with my fearful thoughts? Can you aid me?"

It had been minutes since Sarah had escaped the hooded figure following her from the knoll above the Lady of Sorrows Catholic Church and faced Father Dan, the Catholic priest. He nudged from his deliberations slowly, turned toward the young lady, and asked, "I'm sorry, Miss, what did you say?"

"Nothing, Father, just murmuring to myself," Sarah said quietly, trying to catch her breath. In her embarrassment and exhaustion, she tried to amass what strength she had left.

"You are not one of my parishioners. Have I seen you before?"

"No, I am not from here. I, uh...." Her brown eyes widened and, not finishing her sentence, she slowly slid down the side of the church wall in a faint.

Father Murphy was startled and unable to react in time to catch her as he watched the slender young figure glide gradually to the rustic adobe tiles like a rag doll. He called to one of his parishioners.

"George, please help me! Something is wrong with this young lady. Help me take her inside to the office."

The chubby white-haired man, looking aghast at the young woman, asked, "Who is she, Father Dan?"

"An unsought guest with a cheerless invisible dagger in her soul, I'm afraid. I am certain a startling story will be revealed to us. She wears terror upon her beautiful face, and sorrowful despair. I believe she has withstood a shock, but only time will release the sad tale."

George, shaking his head, helped Father Dan carry Sarah's limp body into the church office. The office was austere with nothing more than bleak white-washed plaster walls with several pictures of icons and a large wooden cross with a silver, poignant Christ hanging from it. Faded Spanish adobe-tiled floors, an ancient, blocky mission desk with an old black phone, several pencils and an empty coffee cup, an uncomfortable wooden chair, and a small settee covered in faded maroon velvet in the corner were all that adorned the office.

Father Dan looked down at the beautiful, sad face of the young lady. He thought to himself, *a terrified waif more heartbreaking none could find.... The lovely child, pallid and bleak, seems as fragile as thin autumn leaves.* He then covered her with a soft wool blanket and sat nearby, reading his Bible.

It was 10 minutes later when she awoke with a terrified start. She sat up and jerkily looked around, her disarrayed auburn hair framing her pale face, a stark image of fear and apprehension. She stared fearfully at Father Dan. The beauty of youth divinely lovely, but obvious panic was framed in the multihued light beaming through tender, joyful stained glass figures adorning a small window in the office. Father Dan could scarce look at her; she was so beautiful and yet so dreadfully pale and afraid. She was still and silent as she searched his face for hope, an anxious frown etched upon her lips, causing her to appear sorrowful. Deep worry lines were carved into her brow.

"Don't be fearful, young lady, you are safe now. I am Father Dan Murphy, priest of Our Lady of Sorrow Catholic Church for over 15 years now. You fainted at the steps of the church door. You seemed to be afraid."

In the multihued light, her exquisite face suddenly smiled. Her golden-red hair framed her delicate face and sweet, sorrowful brown eyes as she sighed. She closed her eyes for a short time and then said in a tremulous voice, "We were running from some people. My friend tripped and told me to keep running... I don't know what happened to him."

"Who were the people from whom you were running?" Father Dan asked as he looked down upon her. He was acutely aware of the anxiety that wound around her mind like a huge python when he asked the question. He felt some icy particle of it himself. It was like snowflakes falling on bare skin, cold and unexpected.

He remembered a dream many winters ago, even once last winter in the flurry of a snowstorm. He was in the throngs of a vague half-fever when he saw something running toward him; it was coming through the mist, dark and evil. He recalled that

Jung characterized it as the shadow, one's own evil self. He looked at the anxious girl and wanted to touch her pale hand in reassurance, a hand that lay rigidly across her breast that was fit for dainty flowers, not colorless unease.

Instead, he asked, "What is your name, young lady?"

With eyes filled with tiny tears from nightmares of the frightening incident, she said softly, "I am Dr. Sarah Addison." She then shuddered. "My friend, Francis, is near the center of the knoll with only the fog and withered leaves to cover his head. He is down by the old stone fence where he fell. He is hurt! Can you help him?"

"Why were you chased? What evil did you see?" Father Dan asked.

She shook her head and tears quietly trickled from her eyes as she looked out the window far away to things unseen, unable to tell him the unbelievable truth. Her beautiful face was lined with ashes of dread.

Father Murphy looked quizzically at the beautiful, fearful face, which seemed to distort into something different, something not understandable. His eyes widened and filled with questions, then he saw her color fade and she fainted once again. She appeared as pale as a corpse, but he felt a faint pulse and nodded.

He crossed himself and retrieved a small, bronze tin with a pewter cross on top, a long colorful silk scarf, and a towel with a cross on it from a drawer in a small desk. He opened the tin, pushed his shaking finger gently inside, and withdrew an oily finger. He made a cross on Sarah's forehead and said a prayer, the last rite. He did it just in case she did not come back from her terror-filled collapse. When he completed the task, her face became peaceful and serene and her unconscious body relaxed.

He did not hear the rustle of leaves outside his window, nor did he see the ebony face hidden under a dark hood, staring with eyes of obsidian through the small stained glass window into his office. He did, however, feel an icy finger touch the nape of his neck. He turned quickly around to face the window, but seeing nothing, rubbed his neck and rose from the young lady's side. He went into another small room so he wouldn't awaken

Sarah and called his friend, Lieutenant Sean Quinn.

"Sean, this is Father Dan. I had a strange occurrence at the church after early mass this morning. I have a young lady here. She fainted near the entrance to the church. George Tanner and I brought her into my office. She is alive, but her pulse is very weak. She said that there was a man that was with her on Keller's Knoll up the trail toward the old cabins. She said the man was hurt. Can you send someone up there to check it out? ... Good, thank you. Sean, please come over here right away. The young lady is in dire terror of something, but she wouldn't say what it was.... No, she is definitely not a homeless lady. She has recently had an expensive perm and her fingers are perfectly manicured, although quite short. She is also slender, but strong and lithe like a runner. She also has a doctorate. I know in these sorry times there may be a few with that high degree that are homeless, but it is quite far-fetched."

He heard, "I'll be there in five minutes, Father!" and hung up the phone.

Father Dan sat down, murmuring to himself.

"Mother of God." He then whispered to the icon hanging on the wall. "What am I to do?"

He went back into his office and felt the warmth of the sun beaming through the stained glass window as it melted the dark cold that had permeated the small room when it had first slithered unwelcome under the door. He glanced at Sarah's now peaceful face as she lay breathing faintly. She was motionless, basking in the warm colors of the rainbow through a spiritual prism from the sun's rays. He scarce could look at her, fearing she might die before his eyes. Worry wrinkled his brow as he paced the small room.

∞

A man, who had seen an injured man on Keller's Knoll about a mile from the church, had called the officer on duty at the station about half an hour prior to Father Dan's call to Sean. Sergeant Cullen and two officers left to look into the sighting of the injured man. After Sean had talked to Father Dan on the phone, he wondered if the man was the same one that had been called in at the police station earlier.

Lieutenant Quinn grabbed his gun and jacket and informed Sergeant Flynn where he was going. He told him to keep in touch with him and the officers who were searching for the injured man on Keller's Knoll. He ran out the front door to his police cruiser. He turned on the siren and the flashing light and sped to Our Lady of Sorrows.

Lieutenant Quinn sped to the front of the church and ran up the adobe-tiled stairs to the massive mahogany front doors. He pulled on the metal rung, opened the heavy door, and called out for Father Dan.

"Father Dan, it's Sean! Where are you?"

"I'm in my office, Sean!" a shallow voice echoed from afar.

Lt. Quinn went across the nave and down a hallway to the office, shook Father Dan's hand, and looked down at the girl.

"Who is she, Father?"

"She said her name is Dr. Sarah Addison. I have never seen her before. After my 7:00 mass it was very foggy, the dawn was just breaking, and I saw a figure running frantically out of the knoll above the church into the light. She had about her a strange sense of silent dread. Tangled in the midst of the dawn I smelled the lifeless breath of crushed buds of roses around her. The yellow wet-leaved path through which her footsteps wound was laced with a sense of apprehension. She disappeared into the midst of the parishioners as they mingled in front of the church. I then saw a strange, hooded black man. I had never seen him before, either. It appeared that he had been running behind her. He came into the clearing, stopped abruptly, and stood for a moment. His hands seemed to be clutching something beneath his cloak. Upon seeing me and the mass of people around the young lady, he slipped away around the corner of the church."

"Hm, that is very odd and, except for your perfumed phrases – probably a carryover from teaching philosophy and literature at the local junior college – it was very detailed."

Father Dan turned a bit pink, looked at the ceiling, then shrugged with an embarrassed smile and looked at Sean.

"You say she is not a parishioner…. I wonder why she came here. You say the dark man under the hood was also a stranger?" he asked as he felt for the lady's pulse. It was steady but still a bit weak.

"That is correct. I have never seen either of them. The young lady eventually came up to me, mumbled something I couldn't understand, and fainted at my feet. I had George help me bring her into the office and we put her on the settee in the corner. I covered her with a light blanket. I went out to look around the church to see if I could find the other person, but by that time, the hooded black man had disappeared. She seems to be sleeping peacefully now. She has no signs of trauma and no wounds. What do you think happened?"

"I don't know, Father, it is all somewhat unusual. Any form of ID?"

"I didn't see any ID, but I didn't look in her satchel, or at the wallet that dropped out. After I put it back, I didn't want to pry any further."

"She is definitely not poor," Lt. Quinn stated as he sat his huge frame down on one of the large mission chairs, making it look small. He brushed his dark hair back over his wide brow and shook his head. "I guess heartache follows wealth and beauty, Father. When the sun ought to shine, it rains instead. Is this all in the grand plan? You know what the Old Testament says about those with wealth? You know the eye of the needle thing," Sean said.

Father shook his head and looked at the ceiling. He started to say something, but Sean had turned around to make a phone call.

"Yes, this is Sergeant Cullen."

"Cathleen, this is Sean. Did you find the man? ... Oh, good. What do you have on him?"

"Nothing definitive yet, Sean, we just arrived here. There doesn't appear to be any indication of foul play, no wounds of any kind, not even any trace of trauma. He appears to have a swollen and blackened ankle, though. He is dressed in a blue serge suit, not the type of garb one wears when traipsing around the forest. He appears to be unconscious. The ID in his wallet states he is Dr. Francis Vachon, assistant director of archeology of the Archeological Archives Corporation. The wallet contains $600 in 100-dollar bills and his driver's license, but nothing else. The odd thing about him is the expression on his face; it is contorted like he was in terror of something. I don't know, Sean... it is very odd. Something strange has happened here, but I don't know what. Doctor Miles should be here shortly and we might have something more definitive then. I'll call you immediately if he comes to, or if the doc comes up with anything. We are going to have a look around the general area now."

"Okay, Cathleen. I'm at the church now, still talking to Father Dan. The young lady mentioned a man that was hurt on Keller's Knoll, too. It has to be the same man. When you are through there, come over to Our Lady of Sorrows and bring Doctor Miles, too."

"I will, Sean. Bye."

∞

Sergeant Cullen clicked her cell phone off and looked at her two part-time officers, Harry Davis and Mike Conner. There was an uneasy silence as they stood over the barely breathing body of the young man. The mist had mostly cleared at the low levels but hung loosely on the mountainside, casting shadows upon the leaf-covered ground as the sun tried to shine through the copse of trees. Cathleen wondered what the people were doing up on the knoll this time of year, especially in street clothes.

Officer Conner crossed himself and fidgeted nervously with his hand on top of his holstered gun, the other hand holding on to a cross around his neck. He frowned and shook his head.

"This insane world grows colder and nearer to the silence from where we all came with every eerie situation like this. Hope itself becomes much fainter without the intensity of justice when evil passes."

"Holy Jude, Conner, what caused that philosophic bit of platitude to come out of your mouth?" Officer Davis asked. "The man isn't dead, Conner. We don't really know what happened here, and we for damn sure can't say that it was something malevolent."

The chubby Catholic officer who was taking Philosophy 101 and English Literature 101 from Father Dan at the local junior college and taking it all to heart turned a bit pink.

"It's just the look on the poor man's face, Davis, it is so filled with terror, so desolate, so lost, like he had been face to face with the devil or some dark evil… it just got to me." He then crossed himself again and sighed.

Officer Harry Davis shook his head.

"How did I ever get paired with a crazy mystic Catholic like you, Mike? Jeez, every case we're on has some weird, bizarre meaning for you, especially since you started going back to college. Why don't you become a Southern Baptist like me and work at the gas station with my dad and me. We don't get into that dark, sinister Catholic stuff."

Officer Conner looked at him and turned red.

"Come on, Harry, you have to admit this is pretty odd. He has $600 worth of bills in his wallet, a nice new suit somewhat torn and scratched due to the brush, and an expensive watch, but nothing has been taken. He appears almost dead but there is no sign of trauma, his hair is barely mussed up, and he has no wounds of any kind. Gosh, except for the fact that he appears to be sleeping, has an odd terrified look on his face, and has a swollen ankle, there doesn't appear to be anything wrong with him. What do you feel about all of that? You can't feel this is normal, can you?

"By the way, how does the Southern Baptist church differ from the 28 other Baptist churches? How would I know which one is the legitimate one? I also *like* going to college! I plan to make something of myself, Davis, and working at a garage and becoming a Baptist is not what I want out of life! I want to be a full-time sheriff for the county. I also like my religion."

Officer Davis turned a bit pink and started to say

something when Sergeant Cullen interrupted and put up her hand.

"Enough, you guys, jeez! This is not the time for debating religious or career differences. Look around and see if you can find anything in the vicinity before the coroner gets here." Sergeant Cullen directed the two officers to different areas as she shook her head and sighed. She took off in another direction to see if she could find anything.

∞

Sean Quinn, the youngest of five, was always asking odd questions. It used to drive his parents and siblings crazy. He was a huge man, being about six feet four, and weighing in at about 250 pounds with very little fat. He was a naïve, docile giant and a kindly man unless aroused to anger, which took a lot. He had a copious amount of thick black hair, blue eyes, and a happy Irish smile.

"Sean, as to your question about the rich and the eye of the needle. My goodness, it has been some time since you have been to mass, hasn't it? It is not just the wealthy who have sorrow in their lives. The poor have more than their share of it, too, probably more than the rich. It's just that the wealthy get sidetracked with material things and need to pray a lot more to keep on track. They have to make sure not to allow their wealth to contaminate them. Greed and the golden deity of money can bring much calamity and despair, but it can also bring happiness and the financial means to help others. To get through the eye of the needle means to get down on one's knees, it is a metaphor. Camels had to get down on their knees to get through the small opening into the walled city." As the large lieutenant shook his head and looked at the floor, the phone in the adjacent room rang. Father Dan left Sean and the young lady and went to answer it.

"Yes, this is Father Murphy... hello? ... Hello?"

"Who is it, Father?" yelled Sean.

"I don't know, I hear breathing but no one is answering," Father Dan called back from the small room.

Lt. Quinn jumped up and went into the room where he

took the phone from Father Dan.

"This is Lieutenant Quinn, who is this and what do you want?"

The breathing continued for a brief time, then a voice mumbled something incoherent and the line went dead.

"I don't know, Father, the line is dead now. Perhaps it was just some nervous parishioner who is ambiguous about coming to you to confess his sins." Sean laughed.

"Speaking of confession, how long has it been for you, Sean? I don't remember seeing you in confession this last Easter or during Christmas."

Father Dan, wearing a mischievous smile, peered at Sean with sparkling eyes. Sean was no longer laughing and had turned a dark shade of red. He looked at Father Dan and started to make his excuse when they heard a noise in the nave and ran to see what it was. The morning sun beamed through the stained glass windows, projecting beautiful colors on the empty pine pews. They looked around and, finding no one, went back to Father Dan's office. When they reached it, they found that Dr. Addison had disappeared. As Sean looked around the other offices, the phone rang again.

Father Dan ran to the room.

"Yes, this is Father Murphy."

"Oh, Father Murphy, I need to talk to Lt. Quinn, is that okay? This is Sergeant Cullen."

Father Dan called for Sean. The lieutenant shook his head, took a deep breath, and answered the phone. The voice on the other end was upset.

"Sean, this is Cathleen, dog gone it... uh... the man disappeared on me. The lads and I went around to various areas to look for clues, and when we got back, Dr. Morgan was sitting on a log wondering why in the devil I'd called him. It was awfully embarrassing. We looked all over the area and found no one. What do you want us to do now?"

"Come over to Our Lady of Sorrows, Cathleen; send your officers back to the station and Dr. Morgan back to his lab. We have a missing person here, too."

Father Dan looked down at the settee where Sarah had lain unconscious, then at Sean. Shaking his head, he contemplated out loud.

"One wonders how a face so intelligent and fair as hers, so terrified and sorrowful, could look upon some evil presence in the eerie darkness of the mist and not wish to stay in the illuminated sanctuary of a church where she would be safe."

"I don't know, Father, and one shouldn't jump to conclusions. We don't know if there was an evil presence. Perhaps the two were just seen by someone in the knoll… you know, in some, er… well, some indelicate position and they just ran away out of guilt. Maybe her look was not one of sorrow but rather of guilt or fear of exposure."

"No, Sean, I witnessed sheer terror in her eyes and saw the hooded stranger myself. I don't believe it was something that simple that caused her to run down from Keller's Knoll. It was something else, something not just impious, but… probably evil. I felt it myself when I first witnessed the terror that had gripped her. Anyway, don't you think it is unusual for two persons to disappear like they did?"

"Yes, Father, I have to admit it is quite strange, and you know I don't cater to coincidences."

After about 40 minutes, Sergeant Cullen came running through the nave and to the office. She was in a rush. Of course, Cathleen was always in a rush and usually slightly off balance. She reminded Father Dan of a thoroughbred yearling, all legs and energy. She spotted Sean and Father Dan and, with a red curl falling in front of her face and somewhat breathlessly, ran into the office.

"Hi, Sean; hi, Father Dan. Anything new on your end? It's a very odd thing, don't you think?"

"Hello, Cathleen. No, I don't think Sean has anything new here, and yes, it is odd. We were just wondering about all that has happened and we both agree it is more than a little odd… it's downright eerie!" Father Dan stated.

"Yes it is quite extraordinary, Father Dan." She then looked over at Sean. "We found the person who called the station; it was old Henry Adams. You know of him. He drinks a lot. He lives in an old, broken down cabin up in the woods; I think it's cabin D. It's about a quarter of a mile down from Keller's Knoll and just about 30 or 40 yards up from where the man was found."

"Hm, old Henry, huh? Isn't he a little on the balmy side, Cathleen?"

"Possibly, Sean, but he definitely saw the man because we found him where he said he was. Besides, I'm not sure he is crazy, he just drinks a wee bit too much like my daddy did. When he drinks too much, he gets peculiar, also like my daddy did," Cathleen stated as she nodded her head and smiled. "But, to be sure, he was not under the spell of the demon rum when we talked to him. He also swore he saw a pretty young lady with flaming red hair running down the footpath adjacent to the main trail he was on. That was about three or four minutes before he came upon the man hidden under a pile of withered yellow leaves. He also said he saw a tall, hooded figure running after the lady."

Father Dan shook his head.

"Well, now we do have a mystery, but I also have another mass coming up and I have to get prepared. I'll see you two later. Say, perhaps you both should stay for mass. I don't remember seeing you often enough at mass lately, either, young lady."

Cathleen turned pink and stammered.

"Er, uh, I've just had a lot to do, Father Dan. Sean keeps me so darn busy, even on Sundays. I can hardly breathe let alone get to mass." She pulled at her red curls, puckered her lips, and carefully started backing out of the office looking at Sean for some help, which she didn't get. He just smiled, enjoying the situation.

Cathleen was too pretty to be a cop, but her father had been a cop and her two brothers were with the FBI, so she figured she would never live it down if she didn't become an officer of the law. She was about five feet seven, weighed about 110 pounds, and had short, curly auburn hair, soft green eyes, and a beautiful freckled face. She was somewhat awkward in a very cute way and always seemed to be in a hurry; she also had an

Irish temper if pushed the wrong way. Sean had found that out the hard way.

Father Dan gazed at her, then at Sean, and nodded his head.

"On God's tranquil ledger our ardent days are marked, young ones. Remember, the debt of gratefulness that begun in our hearts when we were young lads and lassies should be paid in never-ending praises when we get older." Then Father Dan smiled a mischievous and all-knowing grin, staring with benevolent but devious eyes over his glasses at Sean and then at Cathleen.

Sean and Cathleen both quietly moaned and nodded their heads in capitulation. They then headed toward the back of the church. Father Dan smiled as Sean took out his cell phone and alerted the station where he and Cathleen would be for the next hour. Father left to get prepared.

Sean set his phone to vibrate, put it in his top pocket, and glanced guiltily at Cathleen. They both looked like remorseful teenagers who had been caught sneaking out of their confirmation class.

∞

Lieutenant Quinn, Sergeant Cullen, and Father Dan were sitting in the light pine pews after mass, discussing the disappearance of the man and the woman.

"Father Dan, didn't you say the young lady said something when you first saw her?"

"Yes, it seemed to be just soft mumbling, though. I don't know if I can remember the exact words. I think she said something like, 'I have escaped in the reflection of something but for how long? What can I do, who would ever help me?' Or something like that."

"Cathleen, did the man ever wake up and say anything?"

"No, Sean… we thought he was in some type of coma when we first found him. His pulse was very weak and his heart was barely beating, but he got away before we had the opportunity to talk to him."

"Did you or one of the officers find anything in the area?"

"Yes, Officer Conner did. He found a small leather bag about the size of a CD. It was empty and I don't even know if it was the man's. It appeared to be new. Conner rejected the CD idea and said it had to be something in which the man carried some witch's herbs."

"Oh, for crying out loud! Is Conner on one of his dark Irish mystic adventures again? Is his behavior because of your lectures in Philosophy 101, Father?"

Father Dan looked at Sean and shook his head.

"Now Sean, I have no part in Conner's fantasies about the unknown darkness of the universe; he had those thoughts before he ever came to my class. I think it was his Irish grandmother who gave him those ideas."

"Sean, you should have heard him when we found the man; you would have thought the end of the world was imminent!" Cathleen stated with her green eyes wide. Sean shook his head.

"Did you find anything in your office after the young lady disappeared, Father?"

"Yes, by heavens I did! I'm so sorry! I forgot all about it, Sean. It was after we found Sarah missing and right before mass. It must have slipped under the desk. I saw it when I bent down to tie my shoes. I believe it was a business card. It had her name on it, a phone number, a fax number, and the name of a company. I'll go get it. After I saw it, I remembered that a Dr. S. Addison was a famous archeologist. I didn't figure at the time that it was *this* Sarah Addison."

After Father Dan came back with the card, he handed it to Sean. Sean looked at the name, Dr. Sarah Addison, the name of her firm, which was the Archeology Archives Corporation, and fax and telephone numbers belonging to the San Francisco area code.

Lt. Quinn, with a crumpled frown across his wide brow, asked, "What in the devil is the Archeology Archives Corporation?"

"It is a firm involved in archeological excavations all over the Middle East. They excavate old sites and dig up ancient relics."

"Sean, that's the same company that was on the man's ID as well; they had to have been together," Cathleen stated. "The two must be involved in archeology."

"I believe the Archeology Archives Corporation has been awarded over 80% of federal government contracts for such activities in the past few years, much to the chagrin of the universities. They were first contracted by the government to locate the artifacts stolen from the museum in Iraq. That's when I first heard about the firm. They came out of nowhere. I don't think they were even in business prior to that time, which is quite odd for an entity dealing in archeology. Most of the recipients of federal dollars for foreign excavation grants used to be academic archeology departments of universities. The corporation's latest contract was in the news some months ago. The article said they had received a multimillion-dollar contract from the Department of Defense, something to do with a Sudan excavation in the area of Meroe. I believe it had to do with ancient Nubian artifacts."

"Department of Defense? What do they have to do with antiquities, Father, and how do you know all of that?" Sean asked as he wrinkled his brow.

"You forget, my dear boy, that I am an amateur archeologist and follow such things. San Francisco is where the Archeology Archives Corporation is headquartered. I cut out the clipping from a San Francisco paper and kept it. Now, as to what the Department of Defense has to do with antiquities, that I don't have a clue in the world about. It is difficult to understand how relics relate to armaments or wars." He then looked at Sean and said, "God only loaned the world to us in the beginning. In these dire times as in the time of Eden, we must heed what the Lord has asked us to ponder. There are things of more value than wealth and power, and when moral values are forsaken, the apple will fall."

"What the heck does that mean, Father?" Cathleen asked with wide eyes.

"Well, it means those who start and feast upon wealth, power, wars, and other such things will be thrown out of the garden into the darkness of their nightmares."

Too embarrassed to have the good father explain his philosophical allegory further since it still did not make much sense to her, Cathleen simply nodded and smiled. Sean looked at Cathleen then back at Father and smiled, too, even though he had no idea what Father Dan really meant. He wondered what all of this had to do with the Garden of Eden. The three discussed the situation about the missing man and woman for another five minutes as the sun's glaring light finally moved above its ability to shine through the stained glass windows and create rainbows of color. The area turned dimmer as they talked. After a short time, they shook hands and parted.

Father Dan watched the two leave and sighed.

"I don't have a good feeling about the DoD being involved in something where evil is implicated. I wonder what else or who else is involved in this enigma of darkness and subterfuge!" he thought out loud and ambled back to his small office.

∞

About a half hour earlier in an area far from the church, two figures had stopped running. They were panting for breath, one more than the other. Sarah and Francis had met up again after Francis escaped from the police on the knoll and Sarah escaped from the church.

"Did you see the corporation agents and the hooded figure?" Francis asked, trying frantically to catch his breath. "I swear the eyes of the hooded person did something to me and I fainted."

"Yes, I saw them, I don't know what happened to the others, but the hooded person chased me down to the Catholic church. He left when the early mass ended and I mingled with a group of elderly people coming out of the church. I fainted at the feet of the father from exhaustion and dread. I awoke some time later and was lying on a settee. I talked to the father for a short time and then fainted again, and he must have called the police. I was eventually able to get away after a Lt. Quinn arrived and they went to answer a phone in another office. I pretended that I was still asleep. I saw the hooded figure through the window as I lay on the settee and figured I needed to get out of the church as soon as possible. I ran out the back to the field on the opposite side; I don't think he noticed me."

"The phone call was from me. I looked in the window and saw you, the priest, and the policeman. I had just run down from the knoll trying to find you. I called hoping to get both of them occupied. I also saw the shadow of the figure by the side door on the other side of the church; he must have left the window area when he saw you lying on the settee."

Sarah nodded her head.

"It must have been the corporation people chasing us," she said. "They must have followed us after they determined that we had escaped with the scroll, manuscript, and amulet. I don't see how they or anyone could have known about the cabin, though. I also can't see any of the corporation men wearing a hooded cape. I wonder if someone else followed us from the excavation site when we found all of the artifacts and has been tracking us ever since? Remember, we saw a hooded figure near us when I found the amulet and we were discussing the relics. That was while we were sitting on the rock in the evening. I had an unusual feeling at the time. Maybe it's just my imagination again, but I feel something inexplicable is happening here. I just don't know what it is. Did you see anyone else up on the knoll?"

"Yes," Francis replied, "I saw Omar Awad. He is Iranian and works for Daniel Smyth, head of security at the corporation. He is very dark and mysterious and gives me the creeps. I guess he failed to see me as he ran by the area and continued running down the trail. Prior to him passing by, the hooded figure came up to me as I lay hidden under the leaves. His eyes looked down on mine and that was when I passed out. I awoke a few minutes later and that was when I saw another man running by. About five minutes later, as I was trying but unable to get to my feet, an old man came walking down the trail with a shotgun and a dog. He must have seen me sitting in the leaves and heard me moaning. He left immediately and ran back up the trail, probably to call the police since they showed up later. I was able to escape when the police went in different directions. I passed out again after I went about 200 yards due to the pain in my ankle. I fell down a small ravine into some bushes, which I guess hid me from them."

"What do we do now?" Sarah asked in frustration.

"I don't know, I need to think!" answered Francis anxiously, his thin face etched with worry. "We need to determine who to trust, if anyone, first. At this point, we know we can't trust anyone in the corporation."

Sarah nodded. "I don't know anyone in the government that we could trust and the CIA would probably not help us. In fact, they would probably laugh at us." Little did Sarah know how true that was, because CIA agents were also hunting for the two on Keller's Knoll and their orders were to shoot them.

"Francis, my brother is in the FBI. He is stationed in San Francisco, but I don't want to get him involved unless I have to. I may have to later on, but I will wait for now." She leaned against a huge pine tree. "We need someone, a professor in one of the major universities or museums of antiquity to authenticate the items."

"Professor Farah Kaleel at the University of Cairo and Bishop Adamo Bindello at the Vatican are both experts in the field. They might help us authenticate the items and aid in the deciphering of Nostradamus' cryptic poems. I think they could be trusted to keep the items secret."

"Okay, Francis.... All we have to do is find a way to get to the Vatican then!"

Francis shook his head sadly.

"Sarah, we have to get away from here and get the artifacts to the bishop or someone who would believe in us and do something about it, and soon. The relics are safe, right?"

"Yes, very safe! No one will be able to find them. I am wearing the amulet around my neck and I hid the CD, scroll, and the manuscript at the church. They are safe. I don't know anyone who would believe in the things we have, at least not at this time. I have a difficult time believing myself! Anyway, if we gave the items to someone in the media they would probably try to check it out with the corporation or Department of Defense first, and you know what would happen then. The whole thing would go up in smoke, and we probably would, too!"

Francis looked at her.

"What about the father at the Catholic church where you were? Do you think he can help us?"

"I am not sure what a priest would do with this type of data… it would stagger anyone, let alone a religious naiveté. But then again, he might be a historian or have an interest in such things. He is a Jesuit and they *are* the intellectuals of the Catholic church."

Francis shrugged his shoulders and looked at her oddly. He had known many Jesuits when he went to Catholic schools in Paris and he knew that not all were intellectual, but he didn't want to say anything to Sarah.

Sarah nodded and went silent, but the idea still fermented in her brain. She liked Father Dan. He seemed like an intelligent, honest, caring human being and the huge police lieutenant seemed understanding as well. Besides, she had already hidden the Nubian scroll and manuscript in a closet and the disc of the copied ancient Nostradamus manuscript in a bottom drawer in a cabinet in his office. Sarah replaced a disc of Gregorian chants with her disc. She had also left a small note inside the plastic case explaining what was on it if sometime in the future he discovered the switch.

She didn't tell Francis that she had hidden the disc in Father Dan's office or that she had written him a note about what was on it and what to do if something happened to her. She was sure if Francis knew what she had done, he would sneak back and attempt to retrieve the disc. In doing so, it would place him in peril. Francis was not a he-man or even athletic, but he was naively brave.

If she decided to tell the Father, she would call him and

tell him where the disc was or retrieve it herself if necessary. She hoped that she would live long enough to make the call or move the disc somewhere else to keep it safe. She had a desperate dread of the corporation as well as the hooded figure that had chased her. She figured they would hurt her or anyone else who might have knowledge of the relics. She thought that the corporation would be especially ruthless in trying to get back the amulet, manuscript, and scroll for financial considerations. Little did she know that people in her own government were involved in an even darker and more evil scheme and had an even larger stake in retrieving the items. They had even sent black covert CIA agents after them to assassinate them in order to get the items back.

∞

Sarah and Francis walked down the trail strewn with withered orange and yellow autumn leaves. Francis' ankle was still sore and he couldn't run anymore, but he had made a solid wood splint and could walk with the help of a stick.

They watched to see if they were being followed, but failed to see Omar Awad in the dense shrubs on another trail far to their right. Up the trail from him were two CIA agents. They had large binoculars in their hands. The hooded presence seemed to have disappeared. However, as they rounded a corner they heard the pounding of feet and crackling of dead leaves behind them. The two started to run down another narrow deer trail at breakneck speed, which they calculated also went back to the tiny resort town. Francis fell further and further behind and finally, in pain, slowed and stumbled.

Sarah was well ahead of Francis and did not know he had fallen due to the pain. *Sorrow and heartbreak... it seems it is always something,* Sarah thought to herself. *Sometimes when the sun should shine, it pours down rain. Sometimes simple things go amiss. Even in my youth, I confronted others about things they did wrong. Why am I so bent on justice and truth? Why can't I just let things go?*

She came out of her sorrowful daydreaming and noticed that Francis was not behind her. She then heard the crunching of leaves again, and the tumbling of rocks down a cliff. She panicked, but fearing her pursuers, ran faster and faster, fearing the worst for Francis. She finally reached an ancient wooden gate and heard the small city's din buzzing below. She recalled a Haiku poem she had once read:
A private abode
Mid pines and oaks give mute hearts
Happy songs to sing.

∞

Nearby, where Francis and Sarah had been about 20 minutes before, a voice crackled over a cell phone.

"I believe I have located Dr. Vachon. I think he is heading up to a small abandoned gold mine about a quarter of a mile from here. I saw him limping and backtracking up the trail and then to another path; he must have heard me on the trail right behind him. I followed behind him along the path and, after a while, I saw the entrance to an old mine. I believe he entered it. I have not seen Dr. Addison, though. I am not sure which direction she went, but I believe she found another trail and went back down toward the town. What do you want me to do?"

"Go to the mine and don't let Dr. Vachon escape, then wait until Irina and I get there. Turn your GPS on and I will get to your location as soon as possible. If he tries to run for it, you may have to shoot him, but try not to kill him. I will interrogate him when I get there. On condition of escaping severe pain and threat of bodily horror, the thieving traitor will be glad to tell me where the artifacts are hidden and all who know of the plan. There will be little hesitation in telling us anything, even denouncing Dr. Addison, just so he can die peacefully."

"I have turned my GPS on, Omar, and will wait for you," Yide stated, shivering slightly.

He didn't like the tone in Omar's voice or what he'd said about torture. It had been many years since he had killed anyone and that had been justified, at least in his mind, since it was during wartime. He believed that torture was born of soulless men with a deep blackness within their hearts. He didn't like torture and didn't trust the moral integrity of anyone or any nation who used it. He had been sorely disappointed in Dick Cheney when he not only condoned, but promoted the torture of prisoners. He wondered how men of his ilk became leaders of America.

Two covert CIA agents watched Omar and Irina with their binoculars. They couldn't see Yide. They headed back up from the valley. Not too far from the mine entrance, a shadowy figure, face hidden under a hood, watched in displeased silence as the sun reflected off the yellow and brown leaves nestled on the forest floor. He moved silently and stealthily toward the mine.

When Yide made a sound walking on the dead leaves near the partially hidden mine entrance, he took out his gun. Francis, hearing the noise, ran out the entrance of the mine. Seeing the man with a gun, he stopped in his tracks wide-eyed. When he tried to limp away, Yide frowned, sighed, and pointed his gun at Francis and told him to stop. Francis continued limping away. Yide shouted for him to stop again then reluctantly and slowly started to pull the trigger.

Neither of the men heard the twang of a taut string being released with tremendous power, but Yide felt an arrow dig deep into his shoulder blade. He screamed and dropped his gun. His eyes widened and he looked with his mouth agape at Francis, who had stopped. He then slumped over onto a pile of shriveled brown leaves in pain and left consciousness behind.

Francis, seeing the arrow in Yide's shoulder, limped frantically back into the darkness of the cave to escape. He kept hitting the cave walls and tripping on rocks until he eventually saw small rays of light like golden spider webs dropping down a narrow shaft that slithered up to where the light emanated.

He started crawling upwards to the light, fearful and in pain. He clawed at the rocks as he heard rustling in the cave. He knew that someone was chasing after him. In about 15 minutes, after a laborious and excruciating effort driven by extreme pain, fear, and panic, he reached the top of the mineshaft. He escaped from the small hole into the dense brush just as several bats flew out. The fluttering of their wings was the only noise that he heard now.

He fell to the ground, gasping for breath and shivering with dread at what he had seen. He watched in silence from the top of the hill above the cave. He saw a hooded figure come out of the cave and look at the man that was shot with the arrow. He was about 200 feet below where Dr. Vachon crouched above the mine. He saw that the hooded person had a crossbow in his hand.

Francis trembled, found an opening to the left, and started limping in extreme pain down a steep, unfamiliar path.

When Omar and Irina reached the mine, they saw Yide lying face down in a pile of leaves, bleeding and moaning. An arrow was lodged deep in his shoulder.

"What the hell? How could this have happened? Francis doesn't have a bow and arrow! What is going on here?" Omar yelled as he whirled around outside the mine entrance with his pistol in front of him.

After determining that no one was around and not seeing the CIA agents hiding up the trail, they went into the cave and saw that Francis was not there. Omar went outside the cave, opened his satellite phone, and made a call.

"Yes, this is Omar. Francis has disappeared from the mine and Yide is hurt; he was shot—" He was interrupted.

"What? How in the hell did you let that happen? Damn it, Omar, find Dr. Vachon and Dr. Addison now!" Daniel screamed. With that, the line went dead.

"I guess we need to go back down the trail; he will probably head for Clearlake Oaks now. That's probably where Dr. Addison went as well."

"What do we do with Yide?" Irina asked.

"Daniel said to leave him here for now. Give him our water and some power bars. I have to pull the arrow out," Omar stated as he casually broke the arrow's shaft and yanked it from the man's shoulder. Yide screamed in pain, then passed out. Irina poured an antiseptic from her medical kit into the wound then rubbed an antibacterial salve on the injury and bandaged it. Omar looked at the limp body and nodded to Irina. They started back down the trail to town. Irena frowned as she looked back at the body lying in the pile of leaves. She didn't like the idea of leaving an injured comrade behind; lately she was finding she didn't like a lot of things that were going on with Omar or the corporation.

A few hundred feet to the east of the mine on another trail, two CIA agents walked silently toward the old mine. They hadn't seen the hooded figure that shot an arrow into Yide's shoulder due to a curve in the trail. When they reached the mine entrance, they stopped abruptly.

"Now what the hell happened here? Who tried to kill the corporation's security man?" Agent Thomas asked as he saw Yide passed out in a pile of yellow and brown leaves. He had a bandaged shoulder and his arm was in a sling.

"Who knows what those crazy Iranians will do? Maybe they got in an argument and Omar shot him. Omar and Irina probably went back down the trail after Francis and Sarah; let's follow that trail." Agent Ford pointed with his gun, then placed it back in its holster.

Francis was in terrible pain and limping as fast as he could when he saw, from a clearing above a cliff, the small town of Clearlake Oaks below. He was exhausted and in severe pain when he turned a corner and tripped over a tree root in the path. He went tumbling down a slope and hit his head on a rock. Then he continued to slowly tumble down until he hit the trunk of a tree. His eyes rolled in his head and he blacked out as he turned over onto his stomach. He was covered with leaves and out of sight of anyone coming down the path. It was an accidental act; it ultimately saved his life, but added more bruises to his body.

Sarah continued running and eventually saw the sleepy streets of the city below. She tried to reflect upon things other than the terror in her heart, like the soft autumns of long ago. Her mind traveled back in time to a winter amidst the whirl of snow where she softly touched a hand that gave her a small red rose bud. She gave it back to him after she kissed it and said she had to go but would be back to claim the rose someday.

She glanced back and was roused from her thoughts when she saw a figure far above her. She had not seen this person before. He was carrying a rifle with a scope. He was scanning the mountainside but had not spotted her far below the dell. She continued to run and eventually came to a cabin in a cluster of six other cabins on the outskirts of the town. They were all painted forest green and appeared to be forest service cabins.

Sarah knocked frantically on one of the cabin doors and a man with a month's growth of beard appeared on the weathered stoop. On his soft-fringed leather garment, she recognized a rose bud... a faded red rose!

The man gazed at Sarah in shock.

"Sarah, my God! Sarah, how... where?" he sputtered.

Sarah's eyes, which had been filled with sorrowful tears, now held hopeful dreams. She wondered to herself, *could he have heard my crying soul and called me to him?*

Andrew gazed at her terrified face and tear-filled eyes. He thought, *why does she wear the image of utter dread upon her fair face? Why is she in a state of despair?*

"Oh, Andrew, help me! They're trying to kill me!" Sarah whispered, then fainted into his arms.

Andrew looked quickly outside and, seeing no one, bolted the door and lifted Sarah's slender body in his arms. He placed her on the couch in front of the warm fire and covered her with a blanket. He gazed down upon her face and touched her cheek with his hand.

"Oh, my lost Sarah, your face is so bleak and filled with dread but still so beautiful. No being finer exists within this world." He got his 30/30 rifle and a box of ammunition and placed it nearby the fireplace after loading it. He felt Sarah's pulse; it was steady but faint. An innocent smile was etched upon her face. He kissed her soft lips as he brushed away a tear and sat nearby in a chair with the rifle cradled in his arms. He was vigilant, and with a questioning eye, he watched.

∞

He thought back to the past and remembered the brightness of Sarah's face when he'd first met her. It was a vision of beauty and her presence overwhelmed him. Their days together had been sudden, wonderful, and far too rapid, but her short presence in his life had diminished the significance of the world.

It had been years since Sarah was in Clearlake Oaks on a much-needed vacation after she had been on a dig in Egypt. She and Andrew Atkins had met at a turn-of-the-century bed and breakfast in which they were both staying on the outskirts of Clearlake Oaks. They ended up talking about their jobs, dreams, and aspirations, and then of red roses, which were Sarah's favorite.

Andrew was a forest ranger and had been on a short vacation himself; he had just gotten back from being involved in a huge fire in the northwest about 300 miles north of the town and had suffered second degree burns on his arms. They had ended up on many walks hand in hand along the placid blue lake by the town, walking on the pine needle laden trails in the old timber groves. The white-laced trails were sided with lacy ferns and fuzzy dead flowers that were as soft as sheep's wool. They revealed to each other their hopes and dreams and then Andrew was called unexpectedly back to fire duty.

They had gone on a final night stroll when the moon was high and the bright cloud-covered earth was still and white when he kissed her. He gave her the little scarlet bud to wear. While they'd stood in austere silence with strange, muted winter light streaming through her radiant auburn hair, they made a promise that they would meet again. She kissed the tiny beginning of a red rose and then his lips, gave the bud back to him, and said to keep it for her until she returned to him, which was years ago.

In the first six months, they had corresponded weekly, but as she became more involved with her excavations in faraway countries for the next few years, she was unable to contact him because he had transferred to another forest area and she had lost his address and phone number. She had also moved several times to different excavation sites and had a new company phone, so he could not reach her, either.

Andrew went from national park to national park in the northern forests until he eventually moved back to Clearlake Oaks to become the head forest ranger in the area. He hoped that someday he would again meet the beautiful red-haired girl that stole his heart in just a few fleeting days, but after long years moved slowly by, he had given up hope. He now lived in a forest service cabin just outside of town where the moon gleamed on wind-blown jack pines. A yellow path tangled with the shadows of lost dreams, meandered where their footsteps had fallen years ago on snowy paths when they took romantic evening strolls.

Sarah, on the other side of the earth, during warm evenings in barren deserts where nothing hid the earth or the mind from the azure sky tinted by giant moons, often felt the loneliness that followed her into the subtle sadness of the night as she thought of Andrew. Her spirit drifted into unfulfilled dreams and her once clear vision of Andrew faded away until one day, under a spreading water tree, his image was hidden from her forever in the sand-blown chill of an African night.

∞

Francis awoke about 10 minutes after his fall and, hearing footsteps running and getting nearer, crawled further beneath the leaves and pine needles that had sheltered his battered body from view. With his mind in a state marked by extreme confusion and pain, he experienced a shimmer of faces like in a nightmare. They appeared and then disappeared in an instant. He shuddered at his plight and the sinister nightmare in which he and Sarah had become embroiled. He couldn't understand why stealing the relics would cause them to be pursued and marked for assassination. He then heard voices.

"He had to come this way, I see broken branches and the weeds on the trail are all trampled," Omar stated angrily. "Look around. Do you see anything?"

Irina gazed down the slope where Francis had fallen. She saw his pained and fearful face as he lay broken in the bushes. She hesitated and then looked at Omar.

"I don't see anything. What do we do now?"

"Let's follow this other trail. He has to be down there someplace."

The voices faded away and Francis exhaled quietly. He knew Irina saw him and wondered why she had not given him away. Once the agents from the corporation had passed by on the narrow trail, he pushed himself up on his elbows to determine the seriousness of his injuries. He had several new cuts on his legs, which had already stopped bleeding. His arms and face had small cuts and bruises and his ankle was still swollen from his first fall. He also had a small gash on his forehead, but he was not fatally hurt.

In a few minutes, he heard the footfalls of others running down the trail. He concealed himself again in the bushes as they passed. He was not familiar with the two strangers, and after they had passed, he got up, found a branch to function as a cane, and slowly staggered back up the incline and then in the opposite direction.

He figured, even in his clouded mind, that the cabin about a half-mile up would be the safest place to hide and rest for a while. He also craved water since his throat was parched and he was becoming dehydrated. He knew that he could get some food and water at the cabin and put some antiseptic on his wounds. He needed to allow them to heal at least for a few days. He hoped there were some aspirin at the cabin as well since his head hurt and his body ached all over. He wondered if Sarah had escaped and if she still had the precious artifacts.

His thoughts once he reached the safety of the cabin went back and forth between partial consciousness and delirium. He gulped a glass of water then slowly drank another. His mind, puzzled with pain and dread, thought confusedly about the corporation and the American government. The images drifted chaotically while realizations of conceit, greed, and murder flamed in his mind. He thought that when any great nation like America engages in secret and hidden subterfuge, it is like a ship at sea where furious breakers with massive whitening at her lee, senses her last shudder as her helmsman, no statesman of yore, cringes in a darker vision of destruction! America's reputation rests on life's dizzy threshold because of leaders like these, and it ceases being a better world. In his mind, he saw dark storm clouds growing more deadly as they stole nearer to the chasm. He felt that America's gentle spirit was slowly drifting down the dreaded abyss as poisonous leaders took the helm. His thoughts, wearing his soul down, became a dark voice in his mind and he dejectedly fell on the bed and into a deep, troubled sleep.

∞

While Francis slept, the agents continued running down the knoll to the town below and passed the cabin where Sarah was asleep. Andrew kept watch until the bright hours of the following afternoon diminished into an orange dusk. He gazed at Sarah.

How soft I feel this weird autumn evening, while the untamed twilight grips my mind and Sarah slumbers in a fretful dream. The coming moonbeams clothe the majestic pines and pine needle laden trails with scant a desire of clatter! The horizon's eastern contour, lined with many a hushed spire, seems a joyful sight, a string of flame, like the color of Sarah's hair. I stand in awe of my newfound hope in dazzling solitude. Time is breathing gentle expectations into my mind, and as I watch the distant blaze of sun that makes its first leaps of the day, I see only happiness. With those thoughts, Andrew fell asleep.

Unfortunately, Andrew's dreams were to fade into a deafening nightmare and he would have to tell someone about Sarah and her whereabouts, causing him extreme sadness and regret.

Chapter Five
The Vatican

The corporation personnel and CIA agents eventually left the Keller Knoll area after conversing with their various leaders. Sarah was able to recover for a few days at Andrew's cabin and they caught up on their lives with promises for the future. Sarah, as only a gentle flower can through bright fluttering feelings in the sunshine of the morning and the soft embrace of the night in his arms, felt her life starting to renew. She remembered what long lost friends gone apart far too long forget, but with remembrance, her loving thoughts warmed her mind with golden hues. Above her, standing tall with pleased, misty eyes that had been long blind to hopeful tears, was Andrew.

"Andrew, I am going to have to leave again. These last days have been a godsend to me, but I have to authenticate the Nostradamus manuscript. If what I have translated so far is true and the manuscript is genuine, I will have to get to the highest of authorities in the government as soon as possible to warn them. The first thing I have to do is get the aid of some of the best authorities on Nostradamus to look at it."

"Who would that be, Sarah? Are there experts in the United States?"

"I'm not sure, but I don't think so. I will probably have to fly to Rome. Bishop Adamo Bindello of the Vatican is one of the foremost authorities on the writings of Nostradamus. Professor Farah Faleel of Egypt is also an expert in Nubian antiquities as well as Nostradamus. I fear flying back to Egypt, since there is so much turmoil there following the uprising, the fall of Hosni Mubarak, and the election of Mohamed Morsi of the Muslim Brotherhood. I hope that Bishop Bindello can help me at the Vatican."

"I'm loath to let go of you again, Sarah…. You know that I could not stand to lose you again. With you gone the insignificance of my life will become gloomier, and if you don't return, a heartbreaking illusion. I will be sick with an unspoken sorrow to think that I will be without you in the oppressive heaviness of the arrival of each day that you are gone."

"Andrew, be not sad or fearful. I promise this time I will return and our world will consist of taking afternoon walks among the pine copse that surround soft trails of jeweled pine needles and moss. We will sit again amid the singing voices of finch, lark, and robin, and the sorrows born of us now will be no more!"

Andrew drew her near and kissed her eager lips softly.

"Do you think the aroma of rose-leaves or the gentle sounds of birds will cure my heartache? No, only your return will do that. One cannot soothe a starving heart with just the scent of roses. It will be cheerless to wake to empty mornings, sick with the sorrow of your loss."

"Darling Andrew, I do promise to return after my business is through. Remember, I know where you live!" She laughed. "And, if for some reason you must leave, make sure you keep Father Dan informed of your new address."

After Andrew took her to town and they arrived at Lady of Sorrows Catholic Church, Sarah made Andrew leave so that she would not be seen crying. Father Dan opened the door to the office and, standing outside the door was Sarah looking teary eyed and abashed, not at all the fiery red-haired young lady of the past.

∞

After leaving Sarah at the church, Andrew sighed and picked up his cell phone to make a call.

"Sarah is leaving for the Vatican as soon as possible." He hung up the phone and shook his head sadly. He didn't know what to do about his obligation to Sarah and it pained his heart. However, his duty now was to the man on the other end of the telephone. I was a decision that would haunt him.

Back at the church, Father Dan looked at Sarah.

"My goodness, Dr. Addison, thank God you are still alive! Why did you have to leave? You were safe here in this holy sanctuary, my dear. But enough of that, please come inside."

"I'm so sorry, Father. I saw the hooded man who had been pursuing me outside the window of your office. I felt I had to escape and I didn't want to place you in peril."

"Well, dear lady, with God above and big ole Sean and me below, I don't think there was any danger of that, but I am sure you had other reasons, too, didn't you? From what source comes the evil wind that transports you to this place?"

"Father, that is a long story which I will relate to you soon, but first I need to look for something I left with you."

Father Dan, with a smile and a twinkle in his eye, stated, "Yes, quite disturbing to say the least. I started to play my Gregorian chants and lo and behold, I had a very eerie written message about prophecies, Nostradamus, and writings I could not understand instead."

Sarah turned red, pulled his CD of Gregorian chants out of her coat, and handed it to him.

"I felt that was the safest place to hide my disc, Father. I am so sorry I have deceived you so much. I guess now I should tell you the whole terrible tale, but first let me get the scroll." She went to the closet where the albs for mass were hung and reached inside to an old box in the back and took out an ancient leather-bound scroll.

"This is the original of one of the items on the CD, Father. Supposedly, it is a fourth century Nubian scroll. I also have an unpublished book of Nostradamus prophecies hidden in the closet. Allegedly, it can only be decoded correctly with the emerald amulet I have around my neck which is said to be the key." Sarah showed the amulet to the priest, then spent the next few hours explaining the whole enigmatic story to him.

Father Dan listened with incredulity at first, then stared at Sarah after she had finished. He shook his head sadly.

"On the world's earth-floor glows a frightening flame of ice and the existence of a cold chill creeps into the security of the world and our nation. Yours is an appalling tale, Sarah… why would the government and this corporation do such horrible things?" He sighed. "Do you think you have truly translated two of the predictions accurately?"

Sarah looked at Father Dan, shrugged her shoulders, and nodded her head as if to say she wasn't entirely sure.

"To the first question, greed and power. Father, the corporation has made tens of millions of dollars on their nefarious schemes and I suppose they figured they would make billions of dollars more if the other people with whom they are united knew about future catastrophic events. I am not sure what the government plans to do with the prophecies. It is all a mystery and it frightens me. To the second question, I am not totally sure if *any* translations of the Nostradamus predictions are totally accurate, but I figure our translation is close enough. However, we are not sure the manuscript is even authentic yet. The major problem is to get the time and place pinned down. We haven't done that yet. We also need to have the written words and syntax used in the manuscript accurately authenticated by experts in the field as soon as possible."

"Oh, my dear, a new Nostradamus prophecy on the future! If it is true, it could not only make fortunes for the greedy and unthinking corporations, but it could make whoever has it an even more powerful and perhaps more dangerous force than they already are." Father Dan crossed himself. "From a murky, evil darkness the government's skeleton laughs, hides its dead, and mocks the living."

"Father, I am not an expert on Nubian script or Nostradamus' writings, so all may not be lost. I need verification by experts in this narrow field of study. I need to see Bishop Adam Bindello… can you help me?"

Father Dan's jaw dropped and his eyes widened. He grinned and said excitedly, "Oh my goodness, Sarah, God holds us in His thoughts. I am an amateur archeologist and I was going to fly to the Vatican for a series of lectures by Bishop Adamo Bindello, Professor Farah Faleel of the University of Cairo, and many other experts on Middle Eastern artifacts tomorrow. I have two tickets to Rome, but Father Sidney, a dear friend and fellow amateur archeologist, suddenly got the flu yesterday and can't go. You could take his place and show them the scroll, manuscript, and amulet yourself."

"Father Dan, that would be wonderful! I hope that I can trust them not to say anything to the wrong people or tell others about the prophecies!"

"I believe that you can trust their word implicitly. I am sure they would never divulge anything about the relics, at least I know Bishop Bindello wouldn't. However, I am not sure what they might want to do about the Nostradamus manuscript itself. If it is authentic, they might want to claim it for their own separate nations. I would imagine those things could become a dilemma for you!"

"Let's do it anyway, Father. I think it is my only hope at this point. I have another request, too... can you get Lt. Quinn and some of his officers to search for Dr. Vachon in Keller's Knoll again? He is hurt and missing, and I am terribly worried about him. Andrew and I went up the different trails for about five hours during the past few days, but we were unable to locate him or find any evidence of his whereabouts. I know Lt. Quinn and his officers went up there the day before and didn't find him, either, but they didn't find a body so I feel he must be still alive someplace. I just don't know where. Do you think you could get them to start looking for him again?"

"I will call Sean immediately. Er... you aren't going to disappear on me again, are you?" Father Dan said as he gazed at Sarah over his glasses and made his way to the other room.

Sarah turned pink and shook her head as she fumbled with the amulet around her neck. She sighed as Father Dan went into the other room to make his call to Sean. She felt better about things, but still worried about Francis. She couldn't understand where he had gone.

She reached into her pocket, pulled out a dried red rose, and smiled. She was anxiously looking forward to ending her plight into the dangerous game of conspiracy. She was not interested in spy games anymore. Actually, she only wanted to excavate relics and now she just wanted to spend time with Andrew. Unfortunately, that dream would also change drastically in the near future.

Sarah did not notice the hooded ebony figure outside the office that had been listening in on her and the Father's conversation. Father Dan came back into the small office and told Sarah that Sean and three of his officers would be on their way soon to search Keller's Knoll again. Sarah smiled and gave Father Dan a big hug. He held her softly and she cried quietly in his arms. Her fiery temperament had left and only a girl with a load too heavy to bear remained.

∞

It was later that evening that Sean said that they had found Francis hiding in the storm basement of the cabin. No one had noticed the entrance before since it had been covered over with a heavy rug. He didn't respond to the officers or anyone else when they came to the cabin because of his delirium and fear that they were from the corporation or the government.

They banged on the walls and the floor and, hearing a hollow sound, found the trap door to the basement. They found Francis cowering under a heap of old blankets in a far corner. He was disoriented, bruised, suffered gashes, and had a badly swollen ankle… but he was alive. He was in need of medical attention, but they felt he would be fine. He was flown by helicopter to a hospital in Santa Rosa, a large city about 40 miles from Clearlake Oaks. He and Sarah talked on the phone that evening.

"Sarah, I thought that going on site excavations would be academically stimulating and exciting, but not as deadly as they have become. I'm just a simple professor, not a sleuth and especially not a daredevil. I plan to return to my position at the university as soon as I am well. I really don't enjoy running up and down steep, shadowy mountains with horrible people chasing and trying to murder me."

"I understand, Francis, it has been horrible, but knowing what I now know, I must keep going."

"I understand and I am sorry I'm not able to help you anymore. By the way, that hooded individual saved my life. One of the agents from the corporation was going to shoot me in the back when I came out of the mine and tried to escape. The hooded man shot him in the shoulder with an arrow just as he aimed his pistol at me. I glanced at the arrow before I ran back into the mine and escaped out a shaft to an area above the mine. Sarah, it was an ancient Nubian arrow. I don't know why all of this has happened or who the hooded man is, but I'm glad he shot the agent and not me."

"Francis, I am glad that you are okay. You get well soon and don't worry about things anymore. I'm safe in the hands of Father Dan. I'll come and visit you at the university sometime after all of this is over and tell you all about it. I'm going to the Vatican to show the manuscript to Bishop Bindello and Professor Farah Faleel. They will both be at an archeology convention held at the Vatican. Francis… I have to go now. You get well soon, okay?"

"Okay, Sarah. You be careful and don't worry about me. I'm fine and I thank you for the years of extremely important training in excavations. Even with all of the bad things that happened, it was worth as much as my Ph.D."

"Thank you, Francis, for all that you have done, and yes, I will be careful. If I ever get back to working excavations for a university again, I will call to see if you wish to help in some capacity other than being at the digs!" She laughed.

Sarah talked to Francis for a few more minutes and told him she would visit him when she got the opportunity. After hanging up the phone, Francis shook his head and thought about Sarah. *She is gifted with such an infinite thirst for justice. She possesses a dazzling grace honed by years under the blazing desert sun, but is too often visited by a dark ambiguity. One wonders why a person as fervent as she, so tranquil yet so mournful, should abide in such striving for justice; she is obedient to a feverish resolve! I pray no harm comes to her!*

∞

Early the following morning, Father Dan and Dr. Addison were on a 747 on their way to the Vatican. On the same plane were the two CIA agents that had been on Keller's Knoll, and in another row sat Irina Kotov and Omar Awad. They all blended in with the crowd. One of the CIA agents was talking on a cell phone.

A brother at the Vatican, overhearing the conversation between Father Dan and another priest, had informed Darren Williams of the trip. Darren's conversation with the brother had also been overheard vis-à-vis a tapped phone by the director of security at the Archeology Archives Corporation, Daniel Smyth.

"Sir, this is Agent Thomas.... Yes, Sir, she is on the plane just as you were told and it looks like she has the manuscript with her.... Yes, she and the Catholic priest have been looking at a manuscript and she has the amulet around her neck. She believes she is safe with the priest. I personally don't think he could be a threat to a third grader.... Yes, Sir, we will apprehend her as soon as we are out of the airport and it is safe to do so.... Yes, the items will be shipped back via top-secret mail.... No, I haven't seen the people from the corporation.... Yes, Sir."

In the back of the plane was a tall black man in a long, brown friar's hooded cassock. He watched the men from the corporation and the CIA agents, which he recognized in spite of their attempts to blend in. He glanced at Dr. Sarah Addison and nodded to himself. He wondered how the other groups found out that she was on the plane to Rome. He was not aware of another person on the plane who also had an interest in Sarah Addison.

When the plane landed, the black friar got off prior to the others. He walked up the ramp to the main staging room and stood in the shadows until the four came near. He allowed them to pass then followed at a distance. The corporation's security agents went to an entrance to wait for Dr. Addison and the father; the CIA agents trailed behind.

Father Dan spotted an old friend from the Vatican in the hallway. He waved his hand and the priest ran over and hugged him.

"Father Dan, it has been far too long since I last saw you! How are you, my dear friend?"

"I am wonderful, Monsignor O'Brien, and how have you

been? Is your leg still bothering you? I see you still have your cane."

"I can walk as good as ever now, but I still carry my cane for effect. It is too fancy and cost too much to keep in my room. You would be surprised at how much sympathy I get from people, even from the surliest of nuns!" He chuckled. "And who is this, your third, latest, and most beautiful wife?"

Father Dan shook his head and crossed himself.

"Oh, Monsignor, you haven't changed one bit; your Irish humor is as shocking as ever. This lovely young lady is Dr. Sarah Addison, a renowned archeologist. She is taking Father Sidney's place. He came down with the Asian flu the day before we were to leave for Rome."

"Well, isn't that wonderful? Not that poor Father Sidney got the flu, but that this delightful lady came in his place. It is good to meet you, Dr. Addison! It is not often that Father Dan has such beautiful company." Monsignor O'Brien shook her hand. "By the way, Father Dan, I am here to drive you to the Vatican… I drew the short straw!" He looked at Sarah and roared with hearty laughter as he held his ample stomach.

Just as the three were about to walk down to get in the Monsignor's car, the two CIA agents emerged and walked quickly after them. As they reached about 15 feet away, four Italian policemen came running up to them with their guns out. The tall black friar was with them. He was pointing at the two agents and talking excitedly in Italian to the policemen. The corporation security agents took the wrong way out and wound up behind a locked fence, so they couldn't take advantage of the situation. They could only watch what was happening.

The officer in charge replied, "*Questo signore dice che due avete preso il suo raccoglitore, quell vostro fa parre di un gruppo che la gente near dell'abito, prego mette le vostre mani in su.*"

Thomas looked at the Italian policeman and shrugged his shoulders.

"We don't speak Italian, is there a problem?"

The policeman frowned and mumbled, "Silly

Americans." He continued with a thick Italian accent, "This gentleman says you took his wallet and you're part of a group that robs black people. Please put your hands up!"

The CIA agents started to argue, but when the police pointed their guns at them, they put their hands up and watched angrily as Sarah, Father Dan, and Monsignor O'Brien, unaware of the situation behind them, got into a small black Fiat and sped away. While the police were interrogating the CIA agents, the tall black man slipped away into the shadows.

The two men were finally able to show the police their CIA badges, and since the tall black man who had registered the complaint had disappeared, they were released after about 30 minutes. They ran to get a cab, but the other car had disappeared into traffic, which was a nightmare even for those who knew where they were going.

Agent Thomas clicked open his cell phone, shook his head, sighed angrily, and dialed a number.

"Yes, Sir, they got away. Some fanatic told the police we robbed him for some reason.... Yes! ... I don't know, Sir, he vanished into the station somewhere.... No, I really didn't get a good look at him. I only know that he was very tall, slender, and black. He also had a strange accent; it was not European, although he spoke Italian. I would guess that he was probably from some African nation.... Yes, Sir, we will continue to search for Dr. Addison.... An archeology convention? Yes, Sir, that is good information.... No, I haven't seen the corporation people here."

Darren Williams slammed his phone down.

"Damn it, Jon, they eluded your covert CIA agents again. What type of fools can lose a small woman three times? I think you need to do some enhanced training or hire some better agents. Maybe you should use some Darkwater agents, they would have taken care of her by now, permanently!"

"I don't understand, Darren; the two agents I sent are supposed to be among the best. Things out of the ordinary keep popping up that interfere with their actions! They seem to appear for no reason and are totally unforeseen circumstances."

∞

In a cab following Dr. Addison, Omar was on his cell phone with Daniel Smyth.

"Yes, Sir, I think they are the same CIA agents that we saw on Keller's Knoll. I don't know if they know about the Vatican…. Uh, we didn't recognize them in the plane because they were in disguise. We noticed later on who they were."

"Okay, don't lose track of Dr. Addison and make sure you get to her before the CIA agents do. *Your* necks depend on that!" Daniel Smyth said.

He turned around and looked at Maximilian.

"It seems the Pentagon's CIA agents are in the chase again, too; they were on the plane!"

Maximilian rose from his desk slowly, shook his head, and gazed out the window. He turned around suddenly and stared at the executives sitting around the mahogany table.

"I do not like what is happening. We may have to make sure that the CIA agents *and* Dr. Addison are no longer a problem. Daniel, do we have any other security guards that could aid Omar in getting that job done?"

"I'm not sure we have any good guards left who could aid them, but I have a friend who runs one of the security outfits in Iraq. His people are very good and were hired by the Pentagon at one time. I'm sure he has some men in Europe who would do anything for a good stipend."

"Good, contact him immediately!"

Daniel nodded and left the meeting. The others all nodded, except Mary; she was deep in thought. After the meeting was over, she went to her office and secretly made a call to Rome.

"Yes, Maximilian said Dr. Addison is headed to the Vatican and you might have to contend with some new people soon, too…. Yes, Maximilian may hire some private security agents and they could be part of the search for Dr. Addison within a day or so. I will try to find out their names and descriptions as soon as I can and I will contact you…. Yes, be safe." Mary looked around surreptitiously then left the area.

∞

The tall hooded black man nodded his head and made a call.

"Yes, this is Faisal... I have some bad news." After telling the other party the news, he was told to have faith, stay vigilant, and to continue to try to find Dr. Addison before any of the others did.

"Remember what Kahlil Gibran said, my dear Faisal: 'We were fluttering, wandering, longing creatures 1,000 years before the sea, and the wind in the forest gave us words.'"

Faisal shook his head. "Yes, Sire." After he hung up, he said to himself, "The Sphinx spoke only once, and the Sphinx said, 'A grain of sand is a desert, and a desert is a grain of sand; and now let us be silent again.' I heard the Sphinx, but I did not understand." He smiled, nodded, and murmured to himself, "As I do not understand, Sire."

∞

Father Dan and Monsignor O'Brien were discussing past alliances while Sarah half-dozed in the afternoon sun on one of the benches in a serene garden. Beautiful red, yellow, and maroon roses surrounded the garden area and their sweet aroma wafted through the air.

She held the satchel with the relics tightly as she thought about all of those who were after her. Her thoughts traveled to Dr. Vachon and then to Andrew. She sighed and glanced at a stained glass window where the light beaming into the scene magnified some of the prophets. The Vatican loomed far to the left of her, like some medieval castle. Her life had turned topsy-turvy since she went to work for the corporation. She wished she had never been hired.

Following her short spell in the garden after she had arrived at the Vatican, she was summoned by Father Dan. A priest in charge of public relations for the convention took them to an ornate room where several of the convention speakers were sitting quietly, drinking coffee and talking amongst themselves.

Dr. Addison was introduced to two of them. She shook hands with Bishop Adamo Bindello and Professor Farah Faleel then nervously sat down next to them. After the other participants left, Sarah explained her dilemma and the existence of the Nubian scroll and the Nostradamus manuscript. She didn't mention the amulet.

Professor Faleel, a black Egyptian woman, spoke first.

"Dear holy Amentet! Dr. Addison, if what you have said is true and the manuscript can be authenticated, you have the greatest find since the Dead Sea Scrolls. Nostradamus' prophecies have always been thought to be an unfinished work; in fact, centuries 11 and 12 seem never to have been written and the seventh appears to be incomplete as well."

"Professor Faleel," Bishop Bindello stated with some concern. "That may be a little overzealous, saying it is equivalent to the Dead Sea Scrolls, which was a momentous find; however, it would be a very significant find." Bishop Bindello then smiled in a slightly condescending way at Professor Faleel and shifted his chair to face Sarah. "We should go to my office to discuss this further; it is just a short walk from here."

After getting comfortable in Bishop Bindello's office, Farah smiled and spoke.

"As you are probably aware, Dr. Addison, Michel de Nostradame was born on December 14, 1503 in St. Remy de Provence. He was trained to be a medical doctor and obtained his bachelor's degree in only three years and – it is reported – quite effortlessly. He was also proficient in astrology and astronomy, and some believe it is those interests coupled with what some call his genius and gift of clairvoyance that were the main source of his magical inspirations. The book *De Mysteriis Egyptorum* was also considered of prime importance to his research and writings. A Greek neo-platonic philosopher named Iamblichus wrote that book around 340 CE. The exact date, however, is somewhat nebulous. The work was silent for many centuries then flourished during the Italian Renaissance in the 15th and 16th centuries, and a reprint was published at Lyons in 1547. That was when it is believed Nostradamus got hold of a copy.

"We have another connection in regard to what were called the Emerald Amulets of Thoth. It is thought by some Egyptologists that Thoth was the prime architect of the Great Pyramid of Giza. However, Thoth was also mentioned in Egyptian myths as a god with the head of an ibis, which has confused things tremendously. Remember, it was also stated by some Egyptian scholars that the changes in measurements of the pyramid were used for his prophecies as well. If some other historians are correct in their calculations, below the Giza terrain is a system of deep tunnels where the factual history of Egypt, including records and other data, are purportedly inscribed on the 13 Emerald Amulets of Thoth. If only we had one of those stones.... A lot of things might be explained because one of the stones is said to be the key to the translation of prophecies, including all of Nostradamus' prophecies."

Sarah jerked slightly and nodded, but still didn't tell them she had the translation stone hanging around her neck under her blouse.

"If the stones actually existed, my dear professor! All I have ever verified about the stones of Thoth in my research and the research of highly respected scholars is that they are all part of a fundamentally flawed set of myths," Bishop Bindello stated as he looked at Dr. Faleel over his spectacles. "The prophecies of Iamblichus are suspect as well and the date is quite dubious as you are well aware. Some Catholic scholars believe Nostradamus used an ancient witch's practice called scrying to obtain messages from somewhere in the vast cosmos to make his predictions."

"What is scrying, Bishop Bindello?"

"Scrying consists of gazing into a bowl of water to see cloudy images that mysteriously predict the future. I believe the crystal ball is used nowadays, which allegedly gives a much clearer picture!" The bishop laughed heartily.

Dr. Faleel looked at the bishop, frowned slightly, and shook her head.

"Well, as I was saying, Dr. Addison, if we had one of the emerald stones we could have the key to translating the prophecies more accurately and that would be the greatest find ever."

The bishop shook his head again and spoke up.

"Now, now, my dear Professor Faleel, let's not get too excited about ancient myths. We aren't even sure that *De Mysteriis Egyptorum* or the structural changes in the Giza pyramid formed the basis for Nostradamus' prophecies. As for Thoth, his existence and the existence of his emerald stones are unsupported and highly suspect myths. I can't believe that the inscriptions on one of those stones could aid in translating Nostradamus' prophecies. I also can't believe that the variations in the dimensions of the Giza Pyramid have anything to do with any prophecies."

"Dear Bishop Bindello, I am aware that you have a somewhat jaded view of the prophecies in the first place, but one must keep an open mind to such things!"

"Well, Professor, one must remember that it was also said that Nostradamus was an occultist and his practices of divination were considered clearly forbidden by God, and those who participated in such practices would have their souls sent to perdition."

"Are you saying that the early church believed Nostradamus was possessed by a demon?" the professor asked.

"Well, er... possibly! I guess some officials in the church at that time felt he was. But the same prophecies being predicted by architectural changes in the Giza Pyramid appears to be questionable."

"Well, even though that may be moot to some, you know that in 1453 BCE there was the Exodus of the Jews from Egypt, in 1 CE there was the birth of Jesus Christ in Bethlehem, in 29 CE there was the baptism of Jesus Christ, and in 33 CE there was the crucifixion of Jesus Christ. It has been scientifically proven that every one of those events was accounted for by explicit architectural variations or deviations in structural features in the Giza Pyramid as well as the Nostradamus prophecies. The Great

Pyramid, as you are aware, is located at the virtual center of the earth's land mass and Egypt is built upon the Giza Plateau. It all relates to sacred geometry and Akashic records, which were taught in ancient mystery schools. These changes were deemed by experts to be truly predictive prophecies, which foretold each event occurring on those dates. If the Nostradamus manuscript of new prophecies is authentic, there have to be concomitant changes in the structures of the pyramid as well. To check the accuracy of any new prophecies, I need to take the manuscript with me to the Giza Pyramid in Egypt to make sure."

"Hold on now, Professor, next you will want to take the manuscript to Atlantis or get the advice of the Apollonian prophetess at the Oracles of Branchus. I am afraid I cannot accept your hypothesis or your request for the manuscript based on such mythical speculation. I also have a difficult time believing in any of this, especially that the emerald stones were part of the teachings of the mystery schools. Such schools were never even proven to have existed in the first place, let alone all those unfounded assumptions about the emerald amulets. Then again, it appears it is quite difficult for some who seem to be quite educated and intelligent to ignore those things as just myths." He glanced over his glasses at Professor Faleel while giving her a patronizing grin. He then glanced at Sarah, winked, and continued.

"I find that the changes in dimension of the pyramid and the very essence of the epistle of numbers to be a wee bit too much for me to swallow and I am a mathematician; however, stranger things have happened." He gave Dr. Addison another wink and said with a grin on his pudgy face, "I wonder if the idiom 'bird brain' arose from Thoth."

Dr. Faleel snorted, shook her head, and murmured something in her native language at the remark. Bishop Bindello smiled benignly and continued.

"To get back to your request to take the items back to Egypt, Dr. Faleel…. I would much rather do an inspection right here at the Vatican of the so-called new Nostradamus manuscript to see if it is authentic. I don't think I care to have to take a trip to Egypt at this time of chaos to inspect pyramid dimensions or attempt to determine the truth of the basis of the mythical Hermetic teachings of Iamblichus!"

"Yes, yes, Bishop; I realize that you being a Catholic makes you quite immune to myths!" She raised her brow and grinned at the bishop, who frowned slightly. She then smiled at Sarah and continued. "I believe that the Nubian scroll could be Thoth's great scroll of life! Many experts believe that, not only were the Nostradamus prophecies taken from *De Mysteriis Egyptorum*, but that the prophecies from that manuscript were also taken from fluctuations in measurements in the Pyramid of Giza where the emerald stones were purported to have been buried." She smiled at the bishop and continued as she gazed at Sarah. "If that is true, Nostradamus could have found the scrolls at the Giza site and used them to write his prophecies. If we had evidence that some of the prophecies from the scrolls were the same as the prophecies written by Nostradamus, that would give us the proof we need."

Sarah's eyes got wide and she took in a gulp of breath, for she knew that some of them *did*. She and Dr. Vachon had translated a prophecy from the Nubian scroll and found it to be almost identical to one of Nostradamus' prophecies.

Professor Faleel smiled at the bishop and continued, "Nostradamus was known in his days as the prophet of doom because of the prophecies he wrote involving death and war, such as the French Revolution, the rise of Hitler, as well as the Great Fire of London in 1666. As Bishop Bindello has so eloquently stated, and I must admit, many of the interpretations of the prophecies do appear to be somewhat elaborate machinations of imagination. They might also be after-the-fact verbal pronouncements as well, and therefore somewhat suspect. However, hundreds of scholars down through the ages swear by his prophecies. His 942 cryptic poems were called *The Centuries* because they were in sets of 100. A single verse is called a quatrain; there are 100 quatrains in a Century. Even though many generations of historians have attempted to accurately interpret the prophecies, their true meaning has never been translated with

100% surety. I believe this is due to the fact that a key that has not been discovered yet is required."

"Or even 50% surety!" Bishop Bindello stated with a big smile. "And, even if we had the so-called key, we still couldn't be totally positive if anything is accurate. That's because we could not be sure of the key itself! The whole thing is quite a conundrum."

Sarah nodded. "I have heard that Nostradamus prophesized the assassination of John F. Kennedy, and the destruction of the space shuttle Challenger!"

"Well, that appears to be part of the nebulous interpretations," Bishop Bindello stated as he shook his head. "However, whether the prophecies were truly related to those events is rather moot. The unresolved dates and names from his prophecies seem to be, if not inaccurate, at least questionable. A number of historians on the subject feel that many scholars said those were what the prophecies said in order to fit into a true account of history and pay tribute to the genius of his predictive faculty. There will always be those who translate the prophecies to read as they wish, usually related to their own requirements. But, to bring in another conundrum, how does the Nubian scroll fit into all of this unless it is the scroll of Thoth, and isn't he supposed to be a mythical being?"

"I don't know, Bishop Bindello," Sarah replied, "but it appears from a somewhat hurried translation of prophecy number 942 of the Nubian scroll by Dr. Francis Vachon and myself that the scroll contains a similar prophecy to one found in the new Nostradamus manuscript. This manuscript also contained the last four prophecies that have already been published, along with eight new ones."

"My goodness! Now that is fascinating, Sarah. However, it seems reasonable to me that the Nubian Kushite kings were perhaps the ones who actually wrote the prophecies," Professor Faleel stated. "Hm, perhaps Nostradamus actually formulated these later unpublished prophecies from the Nubian scroll as well as *De Mysteriis Egyptorum*, which was published around the same time. Perhaps the writings have the same prophecies as the

Giza Pyramid dimensions."

"I am not really a student of Nostradamus, nor have I ever seen his works until now, if what I have is actually his. The Nubian scroll, according to Dr. Vachon, appears to be authentic. It also appears to fit into the timeline of *De Mysteriis Egyptorum* and is possibly the book Nostradamus used to write his prophecies. I hope that you can authenticate the manuscript and the scroll and determine if the Nostradamus prophecies numbers 943 to 950 are from *De Mysteriis Egyptorum*, from the Nubian scroll, or both. If Professor Faleel is correct, perhaps there are changes that need to be analyzed in the Giza Pyramid as well."

Bishop Bindello's mouth went agape and he stuttered. "That is incredible, Dr. Addison! Since the 16th century the experts have only been aware of *De Mysteriis Egyptorum* and the 942 Nostradamus prophecies, printed in 1568, two years after his death. An ancient fourth century Nubian scroll with the same prophecies would be quite simply amazing. It would turn the archeology world on its head. It might even convince *me!*"

Professor Faleel smiled and looked at Sarah. "If *De Mysteriis Egyptorum* only contains the 942 prophecies, perhaps the Nubian scroll contains the other eight found in the new Nostradamus manuscript. We need to look at the manuscript and the scroll together, Sarah. I believe we can authenticate both. The scroll will be the easiest since it is written in the proper cursive language of the time. It might take even less time to authenticate the Nostradamus manuscript. There are some very specific nuances in his prophetic writings that can be authenticated if the manuscript is his work. We also already know that the verses were written in his trademark ambiguous style with vocabulary in French, Provencal, Italian, Latin, and Greek."

"I think Dr. Vachon attested to the fact that the new manuscript is written in that style," Sarah answered.

"Well, if we can authenticate them we might have eight new prophecies, which could relate to our time. That would be outstanding!" Bishop Bindello stated enthusiastically.

"And perhaps dangerous," Dr. Faleel stated.

After about four hours spent inspecting prophecy

numbers 943 and 944 in the Nubian scroll and the new Nostradamus manuscript, both the bishop and the professor shook their heads in unison. Bishop Bindello spoke first.

"Dr. Addison, we are 90% sure that the Nubian scroll is authentic and unmistakably legitimate. The Nostradamus verse number 943 of the new manuscript, however, appears not to be authentic but the extremely clever work of a highly trained professional forger. We also question the new Nostradamus manuscript's inclusion of only eight additional prophecies when his originally published works were to cover events to the end of time."

"I wondered that about the additional prophecies myself, even though I am not an expert on his work," Sarah commented. "I also wonder about the additional writings in the Nubian scroll after prophecy number 943. I wonder if they are prophecies or just information."

Professor Faleel answered, "Dr. Addison, we would have to translate the scroll more precisely and in detail to determine what the writings say. You may be right; they might not be prophecies. However, getting back to Nostradamus, 943 of his new writings appear to fit the general and historical integrity of *De Mysteriis Egyptorum*, the Nubian scroll, and the published Nostradamus prophecies, but we believe at this time that, at least evaluating number 944, that it has been professionally forged."

"Why a forgery?" Sarah asked incredulously.

Bishop Bindello spoke up.

"What we are trying to say, Dr. Addison, is that prophecy 943 appears authentic, but 944 appears to be forged. The cadence and the words in it just do not seem to fit. The writings appear to be deliberately and totally contrived. We need to examine the other eight to see if the same thing is true in any one or all of them, but we are 80% sure that they will probably all be fake. As to why a forgery, perhaps only the translation of the remainder of the prophecies will give us that answer."

Professor Faleel nodded.

"We are not absolutely sure that the rest of the writings are fake, but we know that prophecy number 943 is real since it is the same as his published works. However, prophecy number 944 is a forgery. That leads us to believe the rest might be as well; it would make no sense to have one fake and the rest authentic."

"But how could number 943 be real?" Sarah asked, somewhat perplexed.

"Quite simple, Dr. Addison," the professor answered. "The forger is an accomplished professional and was able to copy number 943 word for word from the original published manuscript, but 944 just doesn't fit in regard to the use of words and how they are put together. It is fairly simple for an expert to copy something, but to make up something new using a complex combination of words and syntax in different languages is not as easy."

"Yes, quite right," the bishop stated. "However, we would need to set up a set of laboratory experiments and conduct a closer inspection to be 100% sure. If the Nubian scroll's writings are new prophecies, we could be sure. At this point, we are not sure if some of the writings in the scroll are like the ones we have seen in the past. It will probably take us months of careful inspection to translate and decode what has been written."

"Dr. Addison, if someone had just seen and inspected the Nubian scroll, he or she might have accepted that you had in fact found an authentic unpublished manuscript of Nostradamus with eight new prophecies. A professional of the highest order has forged poem number 944. The same is probably true for prophecies 945 to 950. No one on this earth is good enough to put the languages and words together in a perfectly precise manner to fool us, but it could have fooled others. The paper is actual 15th century paper, as is the ink, which confused us at first. It is all extremely peculiar." Dr. Faleel added, "The manuscript is a forgery, but why would someone do such a thing?"

Bishop Bindello spoke with uncertainty.

"Dr. Addison, we also believe there is a possibility that the Nubian scroll is only partially intact. We believe there might be some missing pages. If I remember correctly, a Nubian scroll was stolen from the museum in Egypt last year."

Professor Faleel turned ashen.

"My goodness, Bishop Bindello... how could I have forgotten that? We know that a scroll was stolen. I wonder if this is the same one. I will have to contact the Cairo curator to verify that fact."

"The question is, why was the Nostradamus manuscript forged in the first place? There must be some purpose and it might be determined by translating the prophecies," the bishop noted.

Sarah nodded at the others.

"That is an enigma, isn't it? In relationship to the Nubian scroll, that was all we found during our excavation. If there are more pages, they must be someplace else. Perhaps still at the museum."

Sarah had still not told the bishop or Professor Faleel that she also had what might be the key to accurately decoding the original Nostradamus prophecies, the emerald amulet. She fingered the stone about her neck and was about to say something about it when Bishop Bindello spoke again, this time with authority.

"Dr. Addison, the Vatican must take jurisdiction over the manuscript immediately. Nostradamus was, as you know, a Roman Catholic. And, even though the manuscript is a fake, I believe the Vatican should be the authority to keep it."

"No, my dear bishop," stated Professor Faleel. "It is only right that the manuscript be turned over to the Egyptian government along with the Nubian scroll, which is connected directly to ancient Egypt and may have been stolen from our museum. Besides, Nostradamus was going to be tried for heresy by the Catholic church and was even deemed a witch by some influential religious of the time." She looked at Sarah and smiled.

"It was said that one of his statements was deemed witchery when he made a remark about a sculpture of Mary. It was taken as derogatory and heretical." She then sighed and looked at Bishop Bindello, who was now shaking his head back and forth. She continued, "Nostradamus stated that he was only describing the statue's lack of aesthetic appeal, but his plea was ignored and the inquisitors were going to send him to Toulouse for trial. Nostradamus, fearing a trial for heresy, fled to Lorraine and then went to Venice and Sicily, keeping away from the church authorities from 1538 to 1544. I think it is highly possible that he also went to the southern part of Egypt during that time and that is where he encountered the fourth century Nubian scroll. Anyway, I just don't feel he was still a true Catholic and therefore Egypt should have jurisdiction over the document, and the scroll may be our property anyway."

Bishop Bindello looked at the ornate ceiling above his head and smiled.

"Well, it is quite a moot point, isn't it?" He looked at Professor Faleel and Sarah and, changing the topic, said, "Dr. Addison, from our initial inspection of the documents, the date of the eight new poems in the new manuscript were forged to look like they had been written around 1540 to 1543. However, we believe they were actually written recently, perhaps even this past year or so. We believe that it would be too difficult even for a professional to fake the date-line signature of the writings!"

Going back to the original discussion, Professor Faleel stated, "During those years, Nostradamus could have been in Egypt part of the time, perhaps even in the Giza pyramid. I should take the documents to Egypt to make sure!"

"My dear Professor Faleel, you never give up!" the Bishop snorted. "But back to the ridiculous story about him not being a Catholic. He was eventually taken back into the holy Catholic church and was buried upright in one of the walls of the Church of the Cordeliers at Salon. Besides, Professor, you must remember that the original Nostradamus manuscript was donated to Pope Urban VIII by his son."

"I still affirm that he was not legitimately a Catholic at the time of his death, but regardless of that, we cannot base the jurisdiction of the new manuscript on the fact that the published one was donated to the Vatican or that he may have been a Catholic!" stated Professor Faleel with a bit of hubris. "And since his prophecies are still believed by most experts to be taken from *De Mysteriis Egyptorum,* possibly from the Nubian scroll, and many would argue the Giza Pyramid, that clearly places the new manuscript in the jurisdiction of the Egyptian government, even if it turns out to be a total forgery."

Dr. Addison, attempting to stop the academic and jurisdictional argument and needing further information, interrupted the confrontational discourse and asked a question.

"It was rumored that a secret scroll or document or something was in his coffin. It was supposed to be able to accurately translate his prophecies. Do either of you have information on that?"

Bishop Bindello sighed and nodded his head.

"Uh, yes. When he was buried in one of the walls of the church, a splendid marble plaque to his memory was placed there by his wife, Anne. Anyway, the coffin was moved around 1700 to the prominent wall of the church. It was said that, prior to that time, a priest looked inside and saw an amulet made of green stone around Nostradamus' neck. The year 1700 and other writings and symbols were supposedly etched on it. During the French Revolution in 1771, it was said that soldiers from Marseilles broke into the church and, the next morning, they were ambushed by royalists and killed. The coffin had been opened and it was noted that no amulet was found around Nostradamus' neck and it was not found anywhere in the area. I can't recall if there was ever a report of any type of secret translation being found inside the coffin."

"You say the amulet was never located?" Sarah asked.

"Yes, that appears to be true. Some other church artifacts were found, but not the amulet. Is there a reason you asked?"

"No... uh, I was just interested," Sarah fibbed.

Professor Faleel smiled, thinking about what was said about the amulet. "A green stone, yes... that could have been one of the 13 emerald amulets of Thoth. It was probably the key to translating his prophecies and could have been the aid he used when he translated the prophecies from the other documents. If only we had the stone, we could find out if that was true."

Sarah turned a little pink but simply nodded her head since she wasn't sure she wanted to share that the very stone they sought might be hanging around her neck. Bishop Bindello and

Professor Faleel were so intent on taking control of the manuscript and scroll for themselves that she felt she could not give them the rest of the story. She thought that if they knew she was wearing the amulet, they would demand it, too.

She wondered how she was going to get the manuscript and scroll back when a huge din occurred outside the room. People were running frantically down the halls and yelling. Professor Faleel and Bishop Bindello both instinctively ran out into the hall to see what was happening. Sarah grabbed the manuscript and Nubian scroll and ran out another door to a hallway and into an open garden with a huge fountain in the middle.

∞

In the hallway where the noise originated, CIA Agents Thomas and Ford were struggling against six Vatican security guards. A tall, hooded black man in a friar's robe was pointing at them, saying that they were Takfir Wal Hijara assassins and were sent to assassinate the pope. As the agents were taken away protesting and struggling, Sarah escaped into another area of the Vatican. She was unaware that Omar and Irina were watching her as she ran into the garden courtyard. Omar saw that she was carrying something that looked like the scroll and manuscript.

"Irina, it looks like she has the manuscript and scroll with her! Go around to the other side and I will go to the garden to the west. We should be able to trap her near the entrance to one of the other areas."

When Sarah looked back as she was sprinting toward a vaulted entrance to another set of gardens, she saw a hooded friar. Panicking, she turned and ran toward another entrance just as Omar rounded the corner and aimed his pistol at her back. He was about to pull the trigger when the hooded man appeared out of the shadows and shot an arrow at Omar. He was hit in the shoulder and fell. Sarah glanced back, then disappeared into a hallway and anxiously continued running. Omar looked up at his dark assailant partially hidden by a hood, who stood over him as he throbbed in pain.

"Who are you?" he asked with his last breath prior to passing out. The black hooded man said something, but Omar was unable to hear it. The hooded man inspected the wound to make sure it was not fatal, sighed heavily, shook his head forlornly, and ran toward the entrance where Sarah had been a few moments ago.

Irina was on her cell phone.

"Omar, I don't see Dr. Addison here. Where are you? … Omar, answer me; where are you?" She looked up and saw Vatican security guards running toward the entrance where Omar had run after Sarah. She listened to them yelling.

"It must be another one of them! He passed out and is bleeding from the shoulder. There is a plastic gun by his side and it looks lethal. Make sure the pope is safely locked in his quarters and send five men to guard the entrance. I'm going to call the police chief of Rome immediately."

Irena shook her head as she watched the commotion. When one of the guards glanced in her direction, she quickly joined a tourist group that was being shuffled out of the area. A few minutes later, she opened her cell phone and made a call.

"Yes, it's Irina. Omar has been wounded; he was shot with an arrow…. No, Dr. Addison is gone…. Yes, Sir, Omar thought that she had the manuscript and scroll with her. She had been in a room with Bishop Bindello and Professor Faleel for hours, but since Omar thought he saw her with the manuscript and scroll in her hands, he believes that she did not leave it with them…. Sir, I just overheard a conversation between two of the tourists who said that the Vatican guards had arrested two men. Someone said they were part of a clandestine sect of assassins here to assassinate the pope and they had lethal plastic guns on them…. Yes, Sir, it does sound like they were CIA agents…. Yes, Sir, I will wait for your orders."

Daniel Smyth slammed the phone down and looked at Maximilian and the others.

"Dr. Addison has escaped our grasp again and Omar was wounded."

"What? *How* was he wounded in the Vatican? No one can fool their metal detectors unless they have plastic guns," Maximilian stated.

"Irina said he was shot with an arrow, like Yide."

"Damn, what is going on? Who is the person with the bow?"

"I don't know, Max. But we have another problem: two other people have looked at the manuscript."

"Who are they?" Max yelled.

"Bishop Bindello and Professor Faleel," Daniel stated angrily.

"Is that a problem?"

"I don't know, only Darren would know that."

"At least we still have Irina!" Johanna stated.

"What can Irina do? She's just a lousy female!" David Coopman answered angrily.

Mary Drew and Johanna Klimas flinched and shook their heads as they stared angrily at Coopman. They had always disliked the man, but now it went even further for Mary.

Derek Murray, head of operations, shook his head.

"The two men that were apprehended at the Vatican? I'll bet they were the two CIA agents sent by Ralph Anderson. We are now down to one woman and the person who is shooting the arrows. He must be from another organization involved in finding Dr. Addison and the manuscript. What should we do now? We can't allow anyone else to get ahold of the manuscript."

Maximilian shook his head angrily and made a phone call.

"Yes, I need to speak with Darren Williams, chief counsel to the president…. Yes, damn it, it is of critical importance! This is Maximilian Vogel!" After a few minutes, Darren answered the phone. "Darren, this is Maximilian. It looks like we have been working against each other again," he said sarcastically.

"Not at all, Max! We just sent some agents to back your people up again, you know, some crack CIA agents," he stated nonchalantly as he looked over at Jon and rolled his eyes.

"Why didn't you tell me they were going to Rome,

Darren? We could have joined forces."

"Oh, you know how the CIA is, Max… they like to help, but they want to be apart from the actions of civilians. I just got a call from Agent Thomas. For the second time since they landed in Rome, they have been apprehended… this time by Vatican security. They said a black, hooded friar told the security guards they were there to assassinate the pope. Did your people locate Dr. Addison?"

"Yes, but she escaped again and we have another one of our people down."

"What? Another?"

"Yes, it was Omar; he was shot with an arrow just like Yide was in the mountains. Your group is not using arrows now, are they?"

"Damn it, Max, you know we don't use arrows. What the hell is going on out there? Is there someone else interested in getting the manuscript? I wonder why they're after it and how they knew about it in the first place. I'll get Daniel Smyth to get more CIA agents on the ground in Rome. I'll have them work with Irina this time."

"That would be good. I wonder who the others are who are interested in the manuscript."

"No idea, Max. I'm at a loss, but it can't be good. I'll keep in touch."

"Oh, Darren, before you hang up… we also have another problem. Bishop Bindello and Professor Faleel were at the Vatican and met with Dr. Addison. They are experts on the life and works of Nostradamus and they supposedly inspected the manuscript for hours!"

Max heard a gasp and then the phone went dead. He shook his head and hung up the phone. He looked at the others.

"Darren hung up on me. He sounded like a man shot with a gun."

Darren put the phone back on the cradle and looked at Ralph and Jon.

"We have a major problem, gentlemen. Two experts on Nostradamus have viewed the manuscript."

"Who are the people?" Jon asked.

"Bishop Bindello and Professor Faleel, who are Nostradamus experts, saw the manuscript. This is a very serious problem. They will have to be eliminated if they start a ruckus about the authenticity of the manuscript or talk to the press about what they have seen!" Darren stated coldly as he stared out the window.

Ralph jerked when he heard what Darren said, then looked at Jon who was frowning. They did not like the idea of killing a Catholic bishop, especially an influential one at the Vatican.

"We also have another problem... there is definitely a third party searching for the manuscript."

"That's all we need! Who are they?" Jon asked angrily.

"Maximilian has no idea and neither do I. It looks like we may have to work together with Max's group until we locate the manuscript, scroll, and amulet. We will worry about what to do with them after that."

"How could anyone besides the Archeology Archives Corporation be involved? They are the only other ones who know about the existence of the artifacts!"

"I don't know, but it appears someone else *does* know. It is a conundrum we will have to solve."

∞

While the parties to the conspiracy were discussing the new problems that had arisen, a hooded man was racing out of the Vatican in pursuit of Dr. Addison. He picked up his cell phone and made a call.

"Mona, this is Faisal. The CIA agents tried to kill Dr. Addison again. I had to shoot one of them.... No, he is not dead. I was able to shoot him in the shoulder like Yide. I am now in pursuit of Dr. Addison as we speak. Will you contact Kashta?"

"I can't at this time, I have to be back in a meeting immediately. When you get the opportunity, please contact him. He should be near Khartoum in a short time and in range of the satellite. Please keep me informed when you can! By the way, Maximilian Vogel is incensed, and I imagine that Darren Williams is as well. We also have a huge problem: Maximilian just got word that Bishop Bindello and Professor Faleel saw the manuscript for hours. Maximilian called Darren Williams and told him about the two being Nostradamus experts. I am afraid their lives might be in danger. I will contact Dr. Faleel and keep you posted." Mona sighed and made an immediate phone call.

"Yes, this is Dr. Faleel."

"This is a friend. Are you free to talk?"

Dr. Faleel closed and locked her door and picked up the phone.

"Yes, what is it and who are you?"

"Who I am is of no consequence, Dr. Faleel. A nefarious group knows about you and Bishop Bindello evaluating a newly found Nostradamus manuscript. If you say anything to anyone, especially the press, they will eliminate both of you. You must make sure that the bishop doesn't tell others about it, either."

There was a long pause.

"I don't think that is a problem. The priests in the Vatican are extremely secretive about everything. I don't think the bishop will say anything. Do you think they will try to assassinate us even if we don't say anything?"

"I don't know, Dr. Faleel. If they get the manuscript away from Dr. Addison and initiate their plan, they might. Please stay alert!"

"Yes, I will. Thank you."

Farah Faleel hung up the phone, wrinkled her brow, and thought, *the person who called couldn't have been just an interested spectator. Who was she?* She looked around and called David Addison.

"David, it's Farah. I just got a call from an unknown woman who warned me about a group that knows Bishop Bindello and I evaluated the Nostradamus manuscript. She said they would eliminate the two of us if we air our findings or if they start to put their plan into operation."

"That is bad news! I wonder who it was that called you.

It had to be someone on the inside. Have you heard anything about Sarah?"

"She left the Vatican with the artifacts, so unfortunately I was not able to confiscate them. Two men, rumor has it that they were CIA agents from America, were stopped by the Vatican guard and taken into custody. When the bishop and I went to see what was going on, Sarah left. I'm not sure why, but it could be that she did not want either of us to take the items from her. I believe the capture of the covert CIA agents was a ruse again, just like at the airport. You probably saw the same tall black man at the airport. This time he was in a brown friar's robe. It seems he told security that the CIA agents were there to assassinate the pope. I don't believe he was a Catholic friar. What do you wish me to do now, David?"

"Try to contact Olaf, tell him about the problem, then have him do whatever he can to find Sarah. Maybe it will be possible to find her before one of the other groups does. We cannot allow anyone to injure her! We can't allow the other entities to get their hands on Sarah or the relics."

"Who do you think the black man is?" Farah asked.

"All I know is that he wasn't one of our agents.... Wait just a minute, I have a priority one call."

David listened for a short time, frowned, and then pushed a button on his phone and spoke to Farah again.

"It is all true, Farah; I just heard from our mole. The third party appears to be on our side since he saved Sarah's life, but I still wonder why he is involved and who he is."

"I have no idea... anyway, I will talk to Bishop Bindello and see if he has any desire to say anything to the press."

"Okay, Farah, keep in touch."

Professor Faleel clicked off her cell phone and looked around the area. She then made a call to Olaf.

"Yes, this is Farah. I just talked to David... yes, we have another serious problem. Sarah is safe at this time, at least I think she is. She escaped from the Vatican with the manuscript and scroll. The stupid corporation agent, Omar, tried to kill her, but didn't succeed. A tall hooded friar shot him in the shoulder first with – of all things – an arrow."

Olaf stared at the phone.

"An arrow? Who shoots people with arrows these days? Do we know who he is?"

"No, we don't know who he is or what entity he is affiliated with, but it does appear that he wants to protect Sarah, which is a good thing. Beyond that, we don't know. I have no idea where she could have gone. David said to do whatever you have to do to locate her and keep her safe. Locate the artifacts as well before the others get to them. I looked at the manuscript and scroll for about three hours; the scroll is authentic, but the manuscript is a very professional forgery."

"What? A fake? There has to be a nefarious story behind that!"

"Yes, it appears that the manuscript has been purposely written with a specific set of prophecies that would cause chaos in the Middle East and Israel. I didn't get the opportunity to translate them completely, so I can't say which nations beyond Israel were implicated. The one that we decoded, number 944, predicted the assassination of a prominent Israeli statesman.... Yes, it appears Darren's group will initiate the assassination the prophecy foretells in order to fulfill the new predictions.... Yes, I will keep in touch. Good luck."

Farah thought about Bishop Bindello, and in her mind, saw the portly, humorous, saintly, highly intelligent, and thoroughly naïve man and remembered a line from a poem written by Father James Kavanaugh.

> *There are men too gentle to live among the wolves*
> *Who prey upon them with IBM eyes*
> *And sell their hearts and guts for martinis at noon.*
> *There are men too gentle for a savage world*
> *Who dream instead of snow and children and Halloween and wonder if the leaves will change their color soon.*

She sighed and wondered how people as highly positioned as Darren could prey on the innocence of humanity just to further their power and wealth. She could not understand how people could have such shallow souls to build their worlds on flimsy stacks of filthy lucre. It seemed to be the pernicious malady of the elite in the modern age just as it was in the past.

Olaf, after Farah's call, headed out of the outdoor café and walked along the river, making several phone calls to his contacts, but none of them had seen Sarah.

David Addison called another of his sister's cell phone numbers, but it was out of order like the others. He looked over to another agent in the room who had been doing a search on his computer.

"Did you ever find another phone number for Sarah?" he asked.

"I'm sorry, David… it seems she got rid of her corporation cell and her new cell some time ago. If she has another cell, it's probably a prepaid and, unless she contacts someone's tapped phone that we have access to, we won't be able to trace the call."

David frowned and made another call. A man in a small office deep inside a huge underground headquarters in Santa Rosa, FEMA's regional center for the west coast, answered the phone.

"Yes, this is Don…. Good to hear from you, David! How is the search for the artifacts going?"

"We haven't found them yet, Sir. Dr. Faleel made a good bid for it but was outflanked by Bishop Bindello, who wanted the items for the Vatican."

"You mean that the Catholic church has the items now?" the director of operations of a deeply embedded secret division of the CIA asked optimistically.

"No, Sarah escaped with them and no one knows where she went. Dr. Faleel did get the opportunity to inspect some of the new prophecies, however. It appears the Nostradamus manuscript is a forgery, at least that's what I was told. Anyway, Farah said it had to do with the assassination of a prominent

Israeli statesman. Since the assassination hasn't occurred yet, it appears once the information is given to the media, the prophecy will be carried out. It would indicate to the world that the new Nostradamus manuscript is authentic. Darren and his group could then proceed with the other prophecies that may or may not deal with some more problematic situations in the Middle East and Israel…. That's my guess, anyway."

There was a long pause before Don spoke again.

"Well, now that you know the manuscript is a forgery, you must find it. I am glad at least your sister is still safe. Have you been able to contact her and tell her that we will help her?"

"I have no way to locate her or make contact; all of her old cell phones are out of order."

"Are Olaf and Farah on the task now?"

"Yes, sir, and I will be flying over to Rome tonight. By the way, some unknown entity called Farah and warned her that a group may try to assassinate her and Bishop Bindello."

There was a long pause.

"I see. Did she know who it was that called?" he asked as he frowned and tapped a pencil nervously on his desk.

"No, Sir."

"More intrigue for us, David. Keep me informed and I'll try to see what I can find out from here."

"Yes, Sir, I will."

David Addison sighed, picked a plane ticket up from the desk, and headed out to the airport.

David's boss looked to the ceiling and frowned. Things were not working out as planned… he was not happy.

Chapter Six
Dr. Alfonso Agino Barone Romano

After Omar's shooting, Dr. Addison escaped from the Vatican through a series of hallways. The hooded man left after being unable to locate her on the grounds. He went to his hotel room, took off his robe, placed the crossbow on the bed, and picked up his cell phone.

"It is Faisal, Sire. Dr. Addison escaped from the Vatican with the relics. One of the security guards from the Archeology Archives Corporation tried to shoot her and get the relics. I am very sorry, Sire... I had to put an arrow in him. He was aiming his gun at Dr. Addison's back and he would have murdered her and taken the artifacts if I had not shot him.... No, Sire, I did not kill him.... Yes, I will continue trying to find her. Mona called me and said that Maximilian Vogel was very angry; in fact, she said he was irate."

He listened for a few minutes and then clicked off his phone and sat on the bed. Gentle tears ran down the dark furrows of his ebony face like gray lava and he murmured aloud to himself.

"In a world of beauty, I cannot find a flower whose face seems fair to see. I might suffer even hell and mind it not if there was someone there to wear a flower for me."

He left the room after he prayed and got himself emotionally balanced. After an hour spent searching for Sarah and talking to many people along the Tiber River, he eventually found her by sheer luck along the riverbank. He stood in the shadows across the street from a small hotel, watching.

Sarah had finally stopped running after she escaped from the Vatican. She was completely exhausted; some of it was from running, but it was mostly from dread. She ran to the edge of the Tiber River near where the Mausoleum of Hadrian stood and collapsed on the soft, verdant grass growing along the river's edge. She had no idea that the hooded man had located her again and now stood across the street in the shadows, watching her.

She fingered the amulet around her neck nervously and wondered what horrors lay within the forged Nostradamus prophecies to cause people to kill for it. She looked across to a bridge and, as if in a hazy dream, watched lovers walking hand in hand. She thought aloud to herself, "The wounded on the knoll and in the dazzling pillared Vatican lay tragedies. I have witnessed such madness! None can dare to applaud it with but lifeless silhouettes of once gay flowers. Without principles, they seem to play their ghastly game of terror!

"Dread is snaking tightly around my soul. At the dark touch of their evil, darkness – perhaps even death – may soon dwell in my bosom. On the bridge walk careless lovers bewitched by each other's innocence with no concept of the fear I hold in my heart. Oh, what am I to do? I don't have Francis or anyone to aid me now in this alien place. How did the evil ones find out that I was in Rome, and especially at the Vatican? Only very few knew that fact. Only Father Dan, Andrew, and Francis knew."

She then wondered if it could have been Andrew. She was fearful that the answer was yes. She eventually fell into a haunted sleep, exhausted from running with her constant partner: fear. The amulet around her neck glimmered in the afternoon sun.

It wasn't until 15 minutes later that she jerked awake, felt the amulet around her neck, and nervously grabbed the satchel with the Nostradamus manuscript and Nubian scroll to make sure they were still there. She stared nervously about the area. She was cold and shivered from the chill of the evening as well as an inexplicable apprehension, which covered her with its evil breeze.

She noticed that the crowd had left and only a solitary old man remained. He was dressed in a well-worn brown tweed jacket covered with a large cloak and was gazing at the river about 10 yards from her. She stared at him in fear that he might be one of those who wished to kill her and steal the manuscript. However, when he turned toward her, he bowed, smiled, and tipped his beret. She felt sudden relief. He then turned back around and swung a long, slender fishing pole toward the blue-gray river. She saw a thick line soar up into the pink sky, then plunge down into the languid river.

She watched for a while and the old man looked over to her again and smiled. He said something in Italian, put his pole in a hollow metal holder, and proceeded to tamp dark tobacco into an ancient Meerschaum pipe. Sarah watched for a short time, then picked up her satchel and headed to where the man sat on the grass. She sat down quietly beside him, taking in the lovely sweet aroma of his pipe tobacco. She failed to see the tall black man wearing a friar's robe that had appeared again, peering from around the corner of an ancient hostel.

The old man looked up and smiled a friendly smile. He then frowned as he noticed that Sarah sat in a state of quiet hopelessness, seemingly not knowing where to turn or whom to trust.

He placed a gentle hand on her shoulder and said, *"Osservate avete perso il mio caro, voi vi levante in piedo su una terra no practico, osservante il undertain e solo un fantasma scurio ha rovinato la sicurezza?"* He then looked at Sarah, who was looking at him, shaking her head, and shrugging her shoulders. He smiled again and continued in English.

"Oh, I'm sorry, you probably do not speak Italian. Forgive my confusion. What I said was you look lost, my dear… you stand on unfamiliar land looking uncertain and lonely. Has a dark ghost ruined the security of your world?" Sarah nodded her head and sighed. He continued.

"To watch strange-voiced fishermen must be alien to you, fair one. You must see little here that is familiar or safe to you, and such is the pity. To observe an old and foreign man in a great cloak that follows his disparate lord or observe some cheerless person filled with the darkness of a frightening dream must alarm you. It is so much better to have joyful glimpses of pixie trails where vibrant painted tulips sway with joy and young birds sing about young ladies' color. In my cheerful cottage in the hills where I was born, you could sit next to enormous ruins and braid your golden-auburn hair all day while colorful birds sing here and there and children with rosy cheeks run up and down ancient cobblestone steps to the sound of their happiness."

Sarah sighed with relief and smiled broadly.

"I didn't know a fisherman could be such a wonderful poet! How beautiful your verses are, and how they comfort my lonely and frightened heart."

"Well, besides being an old fisherman, my fair young lady," the old man said as he got up, removed his beret, and bowed, "I must admit that I am also Dr. Alfonso Agino Barone Romano. I was, it seems now 100 years ago, a professor of Ancient Philosophy, Semantics, and languages, primarily Demotic, Egyptian, and Coptic. However, in my later years, I taught Latin when students were into less esoteric things like art and literature. I ended up teaching in classes where there were handsome boys and pretty girls flirting instead of studying!" He let out a hearty laugh. "I taught at the University of Rome la Sapienza for 40 years." He paused and pulled on his fishing rod.

"Do you know that the ruins of the Hadrian Mausoleum are over there?" he asked, pointing to it. "It was built to hold the ashes of our adopted emperors. It was enormous at one time. See the ramp, which winds up the side of the ruins? It coiled all around the tower at one time. The ruins are still there, however Hadrian's ashes aren't, which shows that man survives much less in time than bricks." He laughed his joyous laugh again and continued. "One could reach the building by using the bridge over there. Hadrian actually built it himself. Of course, it has been altered significantly over the ages... thank goodness, since it was a very ugly thing. Under the bridge is a good fishing spot in the cool evenings of summer. But enough of me, what is your name, my dear, and why are you so filled with the dread and unhappiness that I see in your melancholy eyes?"

"I am Dr. Sarah Addison, Professor Romano. I am an archeologist."

"Ah, another student of the ancient sciences. Whence comes the evil wind that blows into your waking nightmares, Dr. Addison? You are too young and too fair to be filled with such sadness and apprehension."

Feeling at ease with the old professor and without thinking about her peril but needing desperately to confide in someone, Sara murmured softly.

"I am being pursued by those who would murder me for what I have."

The old man jerked as if hit by a stone, then frowned and wrinkled his brow. He looked quickly and suspiciously around the area and moved closer to her.

"My goodness, fair one, the quickness of your fearful eyes tells the truth of your sorrowful and dreadful statement. What can I do to be of help?"

"Nothing, Professor Romano… I do not want to place you in peril. Two people have been shot already; they may even be dead. I wouldn't want you to be the third."

The old professor frowned, shook his head solemnly, and took a deep puff on his pipe. He blew the bluish aromatic smoke into the breeze.

"What about the police, can't they be of help?"

"I don't trust any government agency at present, Professor Romano… it is all so very, very complicated. I wish I knew what to do," Sarah stated, all of the bravado and fire of her red-headed flash and pride gone.

"Well, first, you must call me Alfonso and I will call you Sarah. Next, you must come home with me. My children are all grown and long gone from our humble cottage. My beautiful wife, also a retired professor but of the Gregorian University, longs to cook for more than just me. It would be an honor for me if you would come to my home and have dinner with us; then you could explain your terrible dilemma."

Sarah hesitated then sighed and nodded her head.

"I can't… I don't wish to place your life in danger, Professor… er, Alfonso."

"It is *my* life, Sarah. I am an old man and have lived a most magnificent yet risk-free life. I have no fear of death. Besides, I have been praying to Mary to intervene with God to give me some excitement in my mature life." His merry eyes sparkled and he laughed his joyous, hearty laugh once again. "*De Nihilo Nihil!* Nothing comes from nothing, my dear… so I must do something!"

Sarah glanced to her right and saw the tall black man in a hooded robe. His face was like the Sphinx's; it was touched with cold serenity and the immeasurable wisdom of the vast, sere desert. The face also contained a lonesome, brooding, and sad vagueness. She jerked nervously and, with eyes wide, glanced at Professor Romano, who was also looking at the hooded person who had turned and walked away down the street.

Alfonso turned, gazed at her for a moment, and saw the dread in her eyes. He shook his head.

"Dark hooded men and shadows in black robes are not pleasant omens. I take it, dear Sarah, that he is part of the problem? Let us leave this place."

She nervously picked up the satchel, put the strap around her neck, fingered her amulet, and took Alfonso's hand as he offered it to her.

"This is nice, Sarah; I have not held such a soft and delicate hand since my wife was young as you."

Sarah smiled and squeezed his hand.

"I feel safe in your hands, Alfonso. Thank you!"

The two went over to where the professor's new silver 150cc Road Runner Classic motor scooter sat proudly. Sarah got on the back of the scooter, and she and Professor Romano raced up a road, bumping up and down along the cobblestones. The hooded black man watched from the corner of the hotel in a black car that was out of sight.

Alfonso was talking and laughing as he veered here and there up and down the cobblestone streets, with an unfettered, fearless abandon. Sarah felt the wind on her face and the rousing exhilaration of the ride. For a brief moment, she forgot her desperate plight into the perils of darkness and just enjoyed the freedom, excitement, and exhilaration of the ride. She and Alfonso failed to see the black car a few blocks down the street, following them.

The trip continued for about 30 minutes as Alfonso went on narrow cobblestone roads that tenderly held two-storied pristine white plastered buildings. They looked like tall blocks of white marshmallows. The white buildings were scattered with windows filled with singing women leaning out with colorful flower boxes, shaking laundry, smiling, and waving to Alfonso. He smiled big smiles, waved at each of them, and then continued to talk and laugh the whole way to his cottage. Sarah felt like a child again, riding on her grandfather's old bike.

She held on tight to the old man and felt the wind brushing her hair like fairy dust; she was experiencing something that felt delightfully surreal. The cold dread fell from her mind like flakes of snow falling from a tall pine tree in a frozen forest. Sarah closed her eyes and tried to imagine that all of what had happened in the past week was nothing more than a nightmare… then she felt the jiggle of the amulet around her neck and bitter reality took hold of her again; she shivered.

The two continued on the motor scooter for another few miles up into the hills above Rome where whitewashed houses with burnt red tile roofs lined the side of the mountain like beautiful fairytale homes. Sarah was feeling calm again and Alfonso continued to talk and laugh as he sped up the spiraling mountain road. Rome lay behind them like a sprawling, colorful quilt as they traveled further and further up the mountain.

Chapter Seven
Others in the Deadly Game

In the Vatican, Bishop Bindello was talking to a cardinal.

"Yes, Cardinal Giotto, the Nubian scroll was authoritatively genuine, but the manuscript very probably was a forgery. I did not see any other scroll that is supposed to be the key to decoding the Nostradamus prophecies."

"Did you see the prophecies?"

"Yes, I saw the new prophecies… there were perhaps six, possibly more. I am not totally sure."

"You realize the necessity of obtaining the manuscript for the Vatican?"

"Yes, I am aware that it is crucial that we need to locate and obtain the manuscript."

"Do you have any suggestions as to how I might go about that task, Sir?"

The cardinal shook his head sadly.

"My dear Bishop Bindello, I am sorry… that is not my area of expertise. I will wait for your word when you locate the manuscript. And Bishop Bindello?"

"Yes, Father?"

"I don't think I have to remind you that Papa will be very upset if the manuscript is not found and brought to the Vatican for safe keeping. What the forged Nostadamus manuscript, if it is forged, might have prophesized for this age should not be divulged to anyone else as it could plunge the world into chaos. Perhaps that is the plan of those who had the manuscript forged in the first place. Bishop Bindello, we seem to be living once again in a cold and evil time filled with secrecies, subterfuges, and conspiracies. We must have closed lips about this, you and I!"

Bishop Bindello sighed nervously.

"Yes, Sir, I know! I will do my very best to find the precious relics and I will not say anything to anyone."

After a short time upon returning to his cell, the bishop

sat down, sighed heavily, and spoke aloud to a barren white ceiling.

"I sometimes wonder why I ever left my small parish to become a bishop in the Vatican. The once sacred and serene paths through which my footprints treaded in peace are now nothing more than shadowy memories, impossible to retrace. Too many of us were lured by the position and the closeness to our virtuous Papa. Above our heads, the huge, glistening, and welcoming Vatican cathedral ascended into the heavens, glittering and sparkling and promising magnificent things.

"One by one, we fools with grandiose dreams, like noctambulists took our places at the golden altar showered in the mesmerizing light gleaming through prisms of ancient stained glass windows. Like thousands before us with such grandiose dreams, we became lost among the banalities of reality. I wonder if many of their feet have rested yet; mine have surely not! Oh, dear God, forgive me for my sins and guide me to your loving bosom." He crossed himself and then rose slowly and dialed a phone number.

"Yes, this is Professor Faleel."

"Dr. Faleel, it is Bishop Bindello. I would like to talk to you about our, er, mutual problem. Perhaps together we can solve the enigma."

"Bishop Bindello, what about the jurisdiction of the manuscripts?"

"Perhaps we can convince our two leaders that sharing the manuscript would be in the best interest for both of them. We could make sure that no one else gets to them."

There was a short hesitation before Farah spoke.

"Yes, my dear Adamo… I believe that might be the most desired outcome. We should both talk to our leaders."

"Yes. God bless you, and may His peace be with you."

Bishop Bindello thought about what the cardinal said about making sure the manuscript stayed at the Vatican, shook his head, and sighed.

"Thank you, Bishop; may Allah be with you as well. I will contact you as soon as I have word from my superiors."

Farah smiled and immediately made a call to her contact to tell him of the new situation.

∞

After Sarah's escape from the Vatican, a miserable religious named Father Kelly picked up the phone ringing in his cell.

"Father Kelly, my dear friend! I need a favor again. You haven't forgotten that I helped you out of your trouble in the past?"

Father Kelly sighed heavily.

"No, Sir, I haven't forgotten. I realize you gave me a great favor. Will I ever be out of your debt?" the man asked sadly.

"Not until I have a certain manuscript in my hands, my dear disgusting little Father. You must understand that I put myself and my country in jeopardy by helping your naïve bishop get you out of the states. Doing nasty little things like you did is enough to send any other man to prison, and in my opinion, is a special abomination for a religious like you. I'm very glad that I am not a Roman Catholic; it must be a very offensive religion. You were fortunate to be allowed to go to the Vatican and not sent to prison."

"Yes, Sir, I realize that; I am truly grateful and have aided you in special favors over the last two years many, many times," the priest said quietly as a silent, cold anger at the insults being heaped upon him assembled like dead ashes in his mind.

"Yes, you have been a faithful servant, my little pedophile Father, but this favor is a very significant one and one you can't fail in accomplishing. You need to trail Bishop Adamo Bindello wherever he goes. I want you to tap his phone so you can record his conversations as well. He is looking for a manuscript, and if he finds it, I want you to get it away from him."

"How would I be able do that?" Father Kelly asked in desperation.

"I have no idea; use your damn imagination, you stupid pervert! I need it; don't fail me!"

Father Kelly reacted as if stung by a wasp and warm tears

flowed from his throbbing eyes and down his pink, flabby cheeks as he hung up the phone.

"Oh, my dearest, loving God… why don't You just smite me down and relieve me of my miserable life? I am a worthless human being and a hideous disgrace to You, Your Church, and myself. I do not deserve to live. If I could garner the courage, I think I would cease my life." He then fell to his knees and sobbed.

A day later, he had tapped into Bishop Bindello's phone and was listening to and taping a conversation between Bishop Bindello and Professor Faleel. After they hung up their phones, Father Kelly called Washington DC.

"Mr. Williams, this is Father Kelly. I just overheard a conversation between Bishop Bindello and a Professor Faleel. They want to get the Vatican and the Egyptian government to agree to share custody of a Nostradamus manuscript and Nubian scroll and work together to locate it. I would guess if that union occurs there will be many people from the Vatican and the Egyptian government looking for the manuscript."

"Damn it, that's all we need… more people involved. If the bishop forms some sort of group from the Vatican to search for it, make sure you are on the team."

Before Father Kelly could answer saying he couldn't be disloyal to Bishop Bindello any longer, the line went dead. He shook his head sadly, crossed himself, and fell to his knees again.

After a dark hour in tearful prayer, he went to a desk and withdrew a small pistol, sat on his cot, and placed it to his temple. He looked up at the large pewter cross, given to him by one of his faithful parishioners from a small church in Boston what seemed like eons ago.

"Forgive me, Lord, for what I am about to do, but I can no longer live my life of shame and guilt. I am a miserable and horrible blight upon my church, my vows, and myself." He then added, *"Deus miseratum, peccavi, acta est fibula, aeternum vale."*

The sound of the single shot reverberated through the long hallway to Father Kelly's cell like a cannon. Sleepy-eyed priests were jolted from their devotionals and trembled with a terrible recognition as they ran to where the noise originated.

The first priest that entered the small cell murmured, "*Agnus Dei.*" He then fell to his knees crossed himself. He got up and went to a small chest, took out a little silver tin with a cross on top, put a long silk scarf embroidered with red crosses around his neck, and laid a small towel with a cross on it on the desk. He dipped his finger into the thick oil in the tin and gave Father Kelly the last rites while other priests stood in the doorway nodding their heads and crossing their chests in devotion. One of the priests had called Vatican security and the Roman police.

After Father Kelly had hung up the phone with Darren Williams and prior to him committing suicide, Brother Simon Defoe had listened in on the conversation. He shook his head, smiled, and put the phone down just as Monsignor O'Brien entered the office.

"And with whom have you been conversing, Brother Simon? Perhaps your girlfriend?"

"No, Father, you know I do not do those things," Brother Simon answered.

"Yes, maybe other things much worse though, huh?" he said, not smiling this time. "I have noticed that you and Father Kelly have been getting close. Remember, there are other more serious sins than fornication with a woman."

"Yes, Father, I am aware of that," he said icily.

Monsignor O'Brien looked at Brother Simon, whom he was given the charge to take under his wing and train for his ordination in six months. He did not like the shifty-eyed man and left the room with a scowl on his face. Ever since Brother Simon had come to the Vatican, he had been a thorn in Monsignor O'Brien's side. He knew Defoe stole things because he had found some items in the bottom of a drawer in a small dresser in his room. He also knew he drank heavily because he had found gin and whiskey bottles underneath his bed and rum bottles in the space under the sink in the bathroom.

Nevertheless, the Monsignor had to attempt to help him on his way to the priesthood and had to keep his indiscretions secret lest he be seen as being impious toward the man and the church. He thought to himself, *that's how so many bishops get into trouble over their pedophile priests*. To love unconditionally as God directed can become a serious dilemma when protecting and forgiving those who undertake the devil's work. It was a burden only the religious could fully understand. He had a hard time with it at times, but tried to keep his faith strong regardless.

After the Monsignor left, Brother Simon dialed a number.

"Yes, this is Simon… I overheard a very interesting conversation I am sure you will be willing to pay a lot for. Yes, that would be adequate, here's what was said…."

Maximilian smiled after he was told of the conversation.

"Well, well, so Darren has a mole in the Vatican, too, huh? Well, so do I, even though mine responds to money, not duress."

Mary had also tapped many of the phones in the Vatican; she was listening in on the brother and Maximilian's conversation and shook her head. She spoke softly to herself as she wrote down the information.

"I will need to get information about Brother Simon to Farah who can get it to Bishop Bindello; he does not need such a person as a priest in the church. What is happening to the Catholic church in this age? Pedophiles, embezzlers, cardinals who build multimillion dollar edifices to themselves and require money from the churches in their dioceses to pay for them as well as for art, while many of their parishioners go hungry.

"There are also religious thieves who sell information to evil people. Too many corporations aid in starting wars, assassinations of leaders and the religious, violent religious Muslim fanatics who defame the name of Islam, and leaders in high levels of the government who scheme, steal, and lie for their own benefit… dear Allah, what is next?"

She then made a call to Faisal to inform him of the new information.

Chapter Eight
Dr. Romano's Cottage

After leaving the slow-moving river and motoring into the hills, Sarah got off the motorbike and Professor Alfonso Romano pulled it into a small, weathered wooden shed to the side of his house. The shed was covered with an ancient vine growing violet and white trumpet flowers. He stretched his back then slowly approached the front door where Sarah was standing, admiring the ancient yet pristine cottage.

The cottage was a gleaming white despite its age of hundreds of years. It had a faded red-tiled roof and verdant, lacy vines with small horns of purple climbing up a molded chimney and across the roof. A crooked mosaic tile footpath led up to a pale blue door with black straps. Sarah could see that it had been a place where happy children once played with wooden hoops and flat sticks, a home where love and patience dwelt.

Out of a sparkling window partially hidden by a beautiful white-laced curtain, a lovely visage stroked with the gentle hand of age and infinite patience stared and smiled a smile painted by Crivelli or Michelangelo. Her face, heavily lined, was doubtless in the quest for aged serenity but was still handsome, noble, and intelligent. The face emitted an inner calmness bred by years of pious kneeling in prayer and loving care of children and a husband. The woman opened the ancient cottage door and gently and lovingly took Alfonso's hand in hers as she gazed at Sarah.

"*Il mio caro Alfonso, dove avete trovato questa anima bella, questa signora giovane e giusta deliziosa?*" the beautiful elderly lady asked.

"I met her while I was fishing, my dearest Madelena. This is Dr. Sarah Addison and she doesn't speak Italian, dear." He smiled as he looked at his wife, then at Sarah. "My lovely wife was wondering where I found such a delightful and lovely lady."

Sarah blushed and smiled broadly at her generous words.

Madelena took Sarah's hand in her firm yet soft weathered hand that had spent eons of seasons in a garden and spoke in a voice of gentle jest as she twirled Sarah around in a circle.

"My, my, I must admit she is the best catch you have ever brought home from that indolent old river of yours. Now you come inside, my dear! It is getting cold outside and I have a great need to hear your story!" she stated with a perceptive smile.

Sarah smiled and stepped inside the tiny cottage filled with tenderness and peace. She felt instantly safe and secure in the aegis of Zeus and in the presence of her two new benefactors.

"Thank you, Dr. Romano," she whispered as if the cottage were a sacred holy place.

"Sarah, you must call me Lena. I have not been a professor with title for many years; and that old love bear there you can call Alfonso."

"I have already told her that, my dear one. Now can we sit or do I have to stand while my old bones ossify?" He laughed. "Dearest, please pour us all some of that good Chianti I bought yesterday. *Bonum vinum laetificat cor hominic!*"

"Oh, you always have an excuse for drinking your vino, don't you, my love? And now it is to warm your silly heart?" She laughed. "My, my; the excuses you invent are never-ending!"

"Sarah, may I pour you a glass of wine, too? It is very good," Alfonso said with a twinkle in his eye.

"I think I would like that very much, Alfonso," Sarah answered, smiling.

After glasses of the delicate but hearty wine, many substantial crackers, and heady cheese, Sarah decided to call Father Dan at the Vatican and apprise him of her location so that he would not worry.

"Hello."

"Father Dan?"

"Yes, who is this?"

"It's Sarah; I wanted to call you to tell you I am fine."

Father Dan's eyes went wide. He then crossed himself and looked at the ceiling.

"Oh, *Dios Mio*, thank God, Sarah, thank God. A man was shot with an arrow here and the two men who were stopped by the Vatican guards were released. Rumor has it that it was determined that they were CIA agents. Oh, my dear girl, I thought you were taken by someone."

"No, Father, I was so afraid I just ran away. Do you know who the man was that was shot?"

"I overheard a woman with him call him Omar."

Sarah took in a gasp of air.

"Oh, my goodness… he is a security guard from the corporation for which I worked. They were the ones after Dr. Vachon and me in the mountains. I guess they are still after me! Father, it appears the CIA is in on the hunt for me as well. Why would the CIA be after me?"

"I don't know, Sarah, it is a mystery! I would like to come and be with you. Give me the address and I'll be there immediately!"

Sarah hesitated briefly but gave him the address and warned him not to be followed. He laughed and said he would sneak out of the Vatican like a ghost of some past monk in the dreary black of night and hail a cab with a blind and deaf driver.

Father Dan got in a cab a few blocks from the Vatican after sneaking out using a seldom-used exit and told the cabbie not to be followed. The cabbie smiled a toothy smile and sped off like he was on the Le Mans racetrack. He weaved in and out of traffic, bouncing on the narrow cobblestone lanes. The little cab jerked, moaned, and creaked as it sped up and down the narrow, bumpy streets. Father Dan was opening and closing his eyes and intermittently crossing himself while grasping his rosary beads and the door handle. After about 30 minutes, the cab screamed up to the Romano cottage and Father Dan crawled out still shaken, handed over $25, crossed himself, and walked unsteadily to the front door of the cottage.

Dr. Romano opened the door, smiled, and welcomed Father Dan into the house.

"I hope you were not followed, Father."

"I don't think that would have been possible, Dr. Romano… I don't even think my stomach has found me yet!" Father Dan chuckled.

Sarah gave Father Dan a hug, introduced him to Alfonso and Lena, and the four of them sat down in the living room discussing all that had occurred in the past few days.

Outside the Romano cottage, as the sun was meeting the horizon at the end of its daily pilgrimage, a tall black man in a hooded robe sat in the back of a black limousine. He watched for a short time before making a call.

"I have located Dr. Addison. She is in a cottage with two elderly people. Just a few minutes ago, the Catholic priest with whom she flew to the Vatican also arrived. I don't believe he was followed…. No, I don't know if she knew the two elderly people before…. Yes, I will contact you with any new information…. You will be coming here as well, good." He gave the woman his address at the inn. He listened for a short time and then nodded as he clicked his phone off.

He looked at the driver.

"We can leave now, please take me back to the inn."

The black car left and wound back down the curved cobblestone road, stopping at a small hotel about a mile below the Romano cottage. The man got out of the car and disappeared into the ancient building. The driver of the car watched for a short time as the sun set on the horizon and muted shadows enclosed the mountainside like a dark mantle. He then turned on the car lights and slowly meandered down the narrow winding lane to the city of Rome below to await the arrival of the woman.

∞

In Washington DC, Jon Pierce was talking nervously to Darren Williams.

"I don't know where she is now. Our two agents just got out of jail; they had a harder time convincing the authorities who they were this time since they were stopped once before at the Rome Fiumicina Airport. This time their IDs did little good. They had to contact the American ambassador in Italy to get them out of trouble."

"You need to go to Rome yourself, Jon, and take some

more agents if you feel you need them. You must not fail this time! We can't have any more mishaps. I want you to run the show there from now on."

"Yes, I believe that is a required step now. I'll take our plane to Rome tonight. I don't want to get any more agents involved, however. Thomas, Ford, and I can handle it."

"Fine, but make sure it is handled correctly. Too much is dependent on it!"

"It will be, Darren... it will be, rest assured," Jon stated solemnly.

Darren nodded his head as Jon left. Then the phone rang and he picked it up.

"Yes?"

"It's Maximilian Vogel again; he wants to speak with you, Sir."

"Fine, Rosemary. Patch him through to my private line," he stated wearily. "Yes, Max."

"Darren, what the hell is going on in Rome? Irina called, Sarah can't be found, and all hell broke loose at the Vatican."

"Yes, that is true, Max."

"I also heard that a priest named Kelly committed suicide."

Darren almost dropped the phone.

"What...? Did you say Kelly?"

"Yeah, why? Do you know him?"

"Uh, no... just wondering. It just seems odd that a religious would do such a thing. I thought the Catholics forbid suicide, something to do with purgatory, I think. Well, anyway, does Irina know anything else about the suicide? Was there a note or message?" Darren asked quite chagrined.

"I haven't heard."

"I see. Max, I was informed that the Vatican and the Egyptian government might be getting together to search for Dr. Addison and the manuscript. That is all we need, a bunch of Egyptian police and the Vatican guards gumming up the works."

"That's for sure! Can you do anything from your end, Darren? You know, government-wise?"

"Hell no, Max; we aren't even supposed to be part of this deal. I can't go using the force of government beyond the covert CIA agents I have already used to intervene in this problem. It could implicate us. Do you still have someone in Rome?"

"Only Irina; your damn CIA goons already wounded my other two men."

"Max, my men have not shot anyone. Why do you keep saying that?"

"Because your men were there on Keller's Knoll when Yide was wounded, then at the Vatican when Omar was wounded."

"Not true, Thomas and Ford were in custody with the Vatican guards when Omar was wounded. Besides, for god's sake, Max, the CIA doesn't use *arrows*!"

"Arrows again! That was how Awad was shot? Just like Yide, huh? What the hell is going on out there? It has to be a third party! What type of nutty group would shoot people with arrows? What the hell is their reason for what they're doing? I don't like this!"

"I have no idea, Max, I can't see any logical reason for anyone else being involved."

"Okay, Darren; okay. What do we do now?"

"Have Irina get in contact with Thomas and Ford. I'm sending Jon over to Rome to handle everything personally. We need to work together more closely from now on until we locate Dr. Addison. I want Jon to be in charge."

"Okay, Darren, keep me posted," Max stated as he hung up his phone and looked uneasily out the window in his office at the people looking like tiny mice running to and fro on the sidewalks below. He didn't like to have men from DC in charge of the situation now, but he had no choice. He called Irina and told her to get in touch with the CIA agents and work with them but keep private contact with him. He also told her she would be working under the supervision of Jon Pierce.

∞

A day after the chaos at the Vatican and the attempted murder of his sister Sarah, David Addison had attempted to locate her in Rome but failed. It was then that Andrew called him again.

"I just heard from Sarah. She told me that she's okay and to call your parents to tell them she is well and that she had lost their phone numbers."

David smiled.

"Sarah is brilliant, feverishly organized in her work, but has always been disorganized when it comes to her personal life."

Andrew said when Sarah called him and he asked where she was, she told him it would be better if he did not know. She said that way she would be safe. He told David that he'd told her he couldn't understand that type of insanity and that he felt she didn't trust him. He said she hung up the phone immediately.

"Yes, Andrew, we know all of that. Thank goodness she called you. The tap on your phone helped us triangulate her general location. We should know her exact location soon. You have done right by me and Sarah, Andrew, now be patient and have faith."

"David, she said she didn't want to place me in an unsafe position, either. She hung up on me when I stupidly insisted on knowing." There was hesitation before Andrew asked, "Do you think she knows about me telling you about the Vatican?"

"I don't know, Andrew. She's probably wondered about how people knew she was in Rome. I am sure she is aware that only you, the father, and Lt. Quinn knew of her plans to leave. Of course we now know that others found out as well."

Andrew took a deep breath.

"What a cruddy mess you got me into, David. I will probably lose the only woman I have ever really loved. I am not getting involved anymore, do you hear me? Do your own damn spy work from now on!" He threw the phone across the room, smashing it into pieces. David's beseeching words were still streaming from the remnants of the phone and then there was stone silence.

Andrew slumped down in his leather chair by the fire with his hands over his face. His thoughts went to Sarah and their last time together. He couldn't abide losing her again, but he felt she probably knew he had betrayed her and would never forgive him. He couldn't explain about David's legitimate and official intrusion into her life since she had taken the scroll and manuscript. He couldn't betray David's position with a legitimate covert CIA organization as it pertained to the stolen articles. He was between a 100-foot-high brick wall and a chasm a mile deep, neither of which he could fathom. The only thing that was true was that the government's interest in the scroll and manuscript was legitimate. That was the only saving grace in the whole stinking mess.

∞

Two weeks had passed since Dr. Addison disappeared from the Vatican, and then Father Dan disappeared from the Vatican as well. Jon Pierce, corporation agent Irina Kotov, and CIA agents Thomas and Ford had been all over Rome asking questions with no luck. Every time Jon called Darren back to give him their progress, his temper and paranoia got worse.

Maximilian Vogel and Mary Drew had just flown to DC to conference with Darren Williams and Ralph Anderson. They were all meeting in Darren's beautiful, opulently decorated corner office overlooking the Washington Memorial. All four sat in 16th century stuffed English chairs, which sat upon a fourth century Persian rug.

"Darren, Dr. Addison and the priest could not have just disappeared into thin air. What the hell is going on in Rome?! What has Jon said?"

"Max, I have no more data than you do and I don't have any idea as to what happened to them. What about Dr. Vachon? Do you have any word on him?"

"Dr. Vachon resigned from the Archeology Archives Corporation right after he got out of the hospital following the Keller's Knoll incident. He has been back at his teaching post at the University of Paris. I don't believe he knows where Dr. Addison is, either. It may be a good idea, however, for you to put a tap on his phone just in case."

"Yes, we can do that. Ralph, can you handle that task?"

The man nodded and made a call on his cell phone.

The meeting went on for about an hour and then adjourned. Maximilian decided to fly to Rome that very night and Mary insisted that she go along.

∞

A day after Father Dan arrived at the Romano's cottage, Sarah, Alfonso, and Lena were updating him on the ancient writings.

Alfonso stated, "The hieroglyphic cursive writing system was replaced by the Greek alphabet, and later Christian Coptic writing was the norm. It is believed that the last hieroglyphic text was written somewhere around 390 to 395 AD."

Sarah nodded.

"Father, it is an easy task to determine which way to read hieroglyphs."

"How is that, Dr. Addison?"

Alfonso said, "Hieroglyphs will have a person or other item face the beginning of a sentence. For example, if a scene contains a picture of a man or woman seated and facing right, then all the hieroglyphs with a definite front and back would face to the right as well and the message would be read from right-to-left."

"That is very nice, love, but we have a cursive text here. Does it look Coptic or demotic?" his wife asked.

Alfonso smiled.

"Around the time when Egypt was ruled by the Romans, even though demotic was used progressively less in communal life, a number of legendary manuscripts were written in late demotic, up to around 452 CE." He nodded and looked at the others.

"However, those writings as far as we know consisted mainly of graffiti on the walls of the Temple of Isis. Coptic written words using the Coptic alphabet, a modified form of the Greek alphabet, is the final segment of ancient Egyptian. It is the direct successor to the ancient languages of Egyptian hieroglyphic, hieratic, and demotic scripts. Coptic flourished from around 200 to 1100 and the last record of it being spoken was during the 17th century. In my opinion, the scroll that you have is written during that earlier time, somewhere around 400 CE, and it is definitely Coptic."

Lena smiled and sighed.

"Well, my darling, now after your lecture on the three ancient languages, can we start translating the Nostradamus sentences?"

"Yes, but it is important to know in what language the Nubian scroll and the amulet were written because that could relate directly to what is written in the Nostradamus manuscript."

"Do you think that the Nubian scroll, the Nostradamus manuscript, and *De Mysteriis Egyptorum* could all contain similar prophecies?" Father Dan asked excitedly.

"Yes, that is a possibility, Father."

"But then where does the amulet come into the picture?"

"That is a bit more complicated, Father. It could be a Rosetta stone for translating Nostradamus' prophecies. From what Sarah has told me about what Professor Faleel told her, it could be the key to the accurate translation of the Nostradamus prophecies."

"I have heard of one of the Rosetta stones! Wasn't it a huge piece of black basalt slab bearing writings that were the key to the deciphering of Egyptian hieroglyphics?"

"Yes, Father, that is true of one Rosetta stone. It was excavated in Rashid, Egypt in July 1799 by Napoleon's army. It was written in the 9th year of Ptolemy V. The stone is 3 feet 9 inches long, and 2 feet 4.5 inches wide. It displays the identical text in three scripts and two languages, Egyptian and Greek. Because of that, one was able to translate Egyptian hieroglyphics by reference to the Greek alphabet. The amulet we have here is different in nature. However, it still might be able to be used to unscramble Nostradamus' weird script, multiple languages, and jumbled poetic writings into decipherable meanings in conjunction with the Nubian scroll with its now-known language, which is Coptic." Alfonso smiled and looked around; he felt like he was back in his university classroom.

"However, there may be even more intrigue to the story, so please forgive my nostalgic slip into some ancient myths. The Egyptian god Thoth, according to myth, was the scribe of the gods and invented writing. He was usually depicted in hieroglyphics with the head of an ibis, but it is felt that was just an aberration depicted by some overzealous Egyptian painter. Thoth, as explained by the Egyptian priest Manetho sometime during the third Century BCE, was known as Hermes in Greek and was referred to in Hermetic writings. Now, here is the possible tie-in: Thoth was rumored to be associated with the Great Pyramid, ergo the Emerald Amulets of Thoth described in Greek and Roman documents could have originated from the Great Pyramid."

"I am afraid you lost me now. But anyway, what is the relationship between the amulet and the Nostradamus prophecies, Alfonso?" Father Dan asked.

"Well, Father, the emerald amulet could be one of what was thought to be the 13 mythical Emerald Amulets of Thoth. According to many authorities, the Great Pyramid is the entity from which all prophecies originated, ergo the Nostradamus prophecies and amulet as well."

"I have never heard of those things being so intricately related, even though Professor Faleel did mention a little bit about that!" Sarah stated as she nodded her head. "Of course I have not studied mythology that much, but I got an earful from Professor Faleel and Bishop Bindello while at the Vatican. The bishop didn't give much credence to any of the myths."

Lena smiled and gazed over at her husband, who was now deeply into his sermon.

"My dear husband does go off on mythical tangents at times, too, so beware of his mixing of ancient metaphors, so to speak."

"Yes, my dear. Anyway, according to some Egyptian experts, some data amassed from the dimensions in the Great Pyramid prophesied the start of WWI in 1914 CE and the end of

World War II in 1945 CE. It just so happens that the Nostradamus prophecies appear to be identical."

"How did they ever figure that the pyramid prophesized all of that?"

"Well, Father, it was all in the millions of dimensions in the pyramid itself. It all has to do, so some experts state, with sacred geometry. The massive stones in Stonehenge, the gigantic idols on Easter Island, and other such things are said to be part of sacred geometry. Anyway, it seems that these events have been associated with specific architectural changes whose dimensions supported the events occurring on those dates. I can't go into the mathematics of the measurements or the theory behind it, not being a mathematician. Anyway, back to the scroll. If the Nubian scroll initially came from the Great Pyramid, it might have been stolen and relocated in a Nubian pyramid. Of course, that would be conjecture on my part." He gazed around at the wide eyes attending his talk, winked at his wife, and continued.

"However, Sarah, we might just have the basis for all of the prophecies and the Great Pyramid might tie all the items together. Before we start, though, I have to say that I am not an expert on the authenticity of the Nostradamus manuscript, just the literal translation of the writings."

"Alfonso, you don't have to be; the Nostradamus manuscript is a forgery according to Bishop Bindello and Professor Faleel, two experts in the field. What we need to do is translate the prophecies in order to see what the fake prophecies say. That might give us a clue as to how the forgery was to be used."

Father Dan shook his head.

"I don't see how it would be too difficult to translate the prophecies, even if they are in a mix of scrambled languages."

"Well, Father Dan, let me give you one example; I'll get my copy of his published prophecies." Alfonso got up and went to the stack of books in his bookcase. He grabbed a weathered leather-bound volume and came back. "Now, Father, I have both a copy of the original writings and the translation. I will just give you a translation of one in English. 'A ferocious attack is being prepared in Cyprus, tear in my eye, for your imminent ruin: Byzantine and Moorish fleet very great loss, to different ones, the great devastation by the rock.' Now that was simple to translate, but to assign an accurate meaning is another thing. It is quite an enigma!"

"My goodness, Alfonso, no wonder there is such a problem in obtaining an accurate prediction from such a writing. It seems like gibberish after it is translated!"

"You should see the mixture of languages and purposefully obscure style of the original words. It takes a herculean effort just to translate it, let alone decode what it means in regard to a prediction, which is usually almost impossible."

Father Dan shook his head, not knowing what else to say. Eventually, Lena and Father Dan sat quietly, sipped glasses of Chianti, and watched as Sarah and Alfonso started on the translation of the forged Nostradamus manuscript with the aid of the amulet and the Nubian scroll. It was two weeks later when the prophecies had been translated and the four conversed in hushed tones as if the walls themselves had ears.

"Sarah, if we translated and decoded the pieces somewhat correctly, it appears that the first predictions of the prophecies have been fulfilled. The uprisings in various Middle Eastern countries, some assassinations, and the upheaval in Africa as well as the possible collapse of the Middle East peace accord. The sixth one, which we still can't seem to decode properly, appears to be one that is going to involve the bombing of churches of major denominations around March 2016, if we used the amulet properly in determining the correct date. The seventh one appears to infer that Iran or some Middle Eastern country will unleash atomic bombs on Israel in the middle of 2015 or 2016, and Israel will in turn bomb them and other Arab countries." Sarah shook her head in disbelief.

There was a deadly lull in the conversation as Father Dan crossed himself and sighed heavily.

"Are you sure that is the correct translation, Alfonso?" Father Dan asked.

"Yes, I think we translated it properly; what do you think,

Sarah?" Alfonso asked. Sara nodded.

Father Dan crossed himself again.

"Dear God, that means Israel will retaliate with the help of America and the Middle East will be one atomic conflagration. But if these are fake prophecies, it could mean that someone else will be the one starting the devastating inferno in the Middle East to fulfill them!"

Sarah sighed and looked at Father Dan then Alfonso.

"It seems I have stumbled on a conspiracy of darkness involving mass chaos."

Alfonso shook his head sadly in agreement, frowned, and then continued.

"It appears that the eighth prophecy states that mass riots and demonstrations reaching tens of millions will take place all over much of the Middle East due to the bombings, and then hundreds of thousands of riots are predicted to take place all over the Islamic world. It seems the United States will be required to unleash their arsenal on all radical Arab nations to protect America from the tens of thousands of terrorists incited by the bombings. It also states that the president will execute some order called order number 11490. Once again, the exact countries as well as the exact dates are nebulous; however, it does appear that all the countries are Middle Eastern and Islamic nations. I cannot understand why we cannot decipher which exact countries they are or what the exact dates are. All of a sudden, the scrambling of languages and purposeful hiding of the true prophecies within the forged Nostradamus prophecies seem to be getting more intense with each sentence. If these are fakes, they sure are good ones."

Sarah shook her head.

"Dr. Faleel and Bishop Bindello felt that there must have been some malevolent purpose to forge such predictions. It seems they were right. What do you say, Alfonso?"

"Yes, Sarah, definitely. As I said, I am not able to authenticate the manuscript, just translate it. From what I have read, what you say makes a lot of sense. Someone wants the world to believe the prophecies and probably plans to carry the first prophecies out in order to start the war."

"I think you and Sarah need to stop for a while, Alfonso. I am sure you are both getting exhausted from working on the manuscript almost 10 hours a day," Father Dan stated as he yawned.

Alfonso nodded.

"Perhaps if we can translate the rest of the eighth prophecy, we may be able to discover other reasons for the Department of Defense wanting the prophecies."

"I don't think we even need to do that, Alfonso. It appears that someone in the Defense Department, and perhaps in other parts of the government, wants to start a war in the Middle East. They can force Israel, Iran, and other oil-rich Middle Eastern nations to destroy each other so that they, whoever they are, can take over all of the countries with oil. It also gives an excuse for initiating order 11490!" Sarah stated.

"Yes, it makes sense that the prophecy would cause someone to initiate the order," Father Dan stated as he shook his head.

∞

In a hotel in downtown Rome, a female voice spoke.

"I am in Rome; does anyone know what is happening at the Romano cottage?"

"I don't know for sure. They have not come out of the house except to go to the store and get food during the past weeks. I assume they are translating the manuscript's prophecies. I saw Father Dan go out several times, but he came back each time with groceries. I don't think the corporation people or the CIA are aware of where Sarah is yet. Do you want me to go to the cottage?"

"No, not yet, Faisal. However, people are probably narrowing down the location by talking to people. I believe they are probably trying to determine the trail of the old man on the motorbike by locating a person or persons who saw him and a woman riding up to the mountain from the river weeks ago. That could lead to possible buildings they went by on the motor scooter and people in the buildings who know about him. They may have already located such a person and obtained general information as to who he is and what route he takes to go to his home. Eventually, they will isolate cottages within the general area where Sarah is located. Keep your eyes and ears open, Faisal."

"Yes, I will keep watch outside to see if anyone appears. I do believe that we need to act fairly soon, though, even before the others find the cottage, if they do."

"Yes, I agree; I will contact you."

∞

In another place, Daniel Smyth and Maximilian were talking to Jon while Mary Drew was in her bedroom listening.

"Are you sure the lady on the back of the motor scooter was Dr. Addison?"

"No, we can't say for sure, but by talking to people in the areas within close proximity to the Vatican and the Tiber River, we narrowed her initial location to the edge of the river near the Mausoleum of Hadrian. That was a little over two weeks ago. When we talked to about 12 people in the area near the bridge, we learned of an old fisherman named Alfonso. We did not get a last name or find out who he is. All we know is that he is known to frequent that area to fish. Some others noted his proximity to a young lady with curly red hair. Two of the witnesses stated they saw an elderly man and a young woman take off on a silver motor scooter toward the mountains. After talking to many women in buildings along the possible routes, we feel we have the general area where Alfonso lives and Sarah is held up."

"What have you been doing since then?"

"I have had everyone canvassing the cottages within a two mile area in the mountains, but haven't seen the old man on a motor scooter or Dr. Addison yet."

"Okay. Keep doing what you're doing and talk directly to the people in all of the cottages in the area. One of them must know where an old fisherman named Alfonso lives. Let me talk to Irina."

"Irina, you speak Italian, don't you?"

"Yes, although it is a little rusty."

"I don't see that as a problem. Go with the others when they talk to the people; they may be saying something that is being lost in translation." He then whispered to Irina, "See if you can get some information that the CIA people can't." With that, he turned and gazed out the window at the Vatican across the way as the other two left the room.

A lady in the adjoining room removed a black device from the wall and sighed. She then looked around and made a call to Egypt.

"Yes, this is Mona. May I speak with Him?"

"Yes, my dear, what do you have for me?" Kashta whispered softly in a bass voice.

"Sire, the other players are getting close to locating the cottage and Faisal needs instructions as to what to do at this point."

"I am sure your wisdom is as great as mine, Mona, but I might humbly suggest that in one more nighttime send Faisal to the cottage and have him inform them they have to leave. Also, ask Sarah if one of the prophecies has been translated to say that major Islamic, Christian churches, even the Vatican and Jewish synagogues all over the world are to be bombed by radical terrorists. Mona, convince Sarah that we are here to protect her, but we will eventually need the Nubian scroll and amulet back in our care. Tell her she may keep the Nostradamus manuscript to give to some high level authorities to prevent the chaos that has been falsely predicted."

"And Sire, if she will not give them up?"

"Then tell her of the extreme danger the others hold for them and that they will be coming for them very soon and she needs to leave with you."

"And Sire, if she will not do that?"

"Then simply tell Sarah that we will still protect her, but that she will need to leave the cottage immediately with the items.

Tell her we will take her and Father Dan to a safe place."

Mona decided not to ask further questions and called Leila and asked her to tell Faisal of the pharaoh king's instructions.

After hearing the instructions from Leila, Faisal said, "I will wait then. What about Mona, what is she doing now? Is she safe?"

"She is monitoring the CIA agents and the security people from the corporation through Maximilian. She does not believe that Maximilian or any of the others know of her affiliation. She also said that there is another deeply hidden spy in their midst."

"What? There is another spy in the corporation or in Darren's group? Does she know who it is?" Faisal asked.

"Mona didn't know; she said she only knows of the person's existence because of a conversation between the person and a person called David," Leila answered.

"Did she recognize the voice?"

"No, she said she could only understand the words."

"And what have you heard about what Professor Faleel and Bishop Bindello are doing now?"

"She is attempting to set up a mutual agreement with Bishop Bindello. She says he is a good man even though he is a Roman Catholic and somewhat naïve to the evil machinations of the people in the world. We could stand allowing the Vatican or Professor Faleel and the Egyptian government getting hold of the items until we can get them back, but we cannot allow the Pentagon to get hold of the items for treacherous chaotic purposes or the covetous Archeology Archives Corporation for greedy purposes. I have also been informed that we have another problem. There may be other private agents who are involved now and they are searching for Sarah and the manuscript, too."

She heard Faisal sigh heavily.

"Leila, I still don't know how the Americans stole the Nubian scroll from the museum or the amulet from the cache inside the wall of one of the networks of tunnels in the Giza Pyramid where it was hidden for seven decades. We must have a disbeliever in our midst who told them of the amulet and then sold it to them.

"I hope that is not true, but even a virtuous sage-king filled with wisdom and knowledge can be mistaken about people sometimes. I think that even some Christians believed that Christ made some mistakes, like the flogging of the moneychangers in the temple. It showed a side to God that was just too human!"

"Yes, Kashta XIII agrees with that premise, too. He also says that everything will turn out well if we believe. Anyway, keep your vigilance and act quickly prior to the assigned day if someone locates Sarah."

"I need to bring my arrows then?"

"Yes, I'm afraid so. Take whatever initiative you feel is right if that happens! Bring Pianki with you as well. Try your utmost not to kill!"

"We will try to take the right initiative."

"Who is to take the right initiative, Mary?" Maximilian asked harshly as he entered her hotel room, overhearing her last sentence on the phone.

Mary Drew straightened as she hung up the phone then gathered her composure quickly, turned around, and said, "I was just taking to Irina; she may have a lead."

Maximilian wrinkled his brow then nodded and walked out of the room. Mary sat down on the bed, breathing heavily as she tried to regain her composure. She started to get up, but as she turned around, Maximilian was standing in the doorway again. This time he had a silver 38 caliber Smith and Wesson pointed at her.

"Maximilian, what are you doing?" she asked, attempting to allay her panic.

"I just talked to Irina about five minutes ago. She said she would be out of phone contact for about an hour and all calls would go directly to Jon Pierce. Now, tell me how it is that you talked to her?"

Mary got up slowly and casually shrugged her shoulders.

"Okay, okay, so I was talking to my lover. Why does that warrant you pointing that ugly gun at me? What is the problem, Maximilian?"

Maximilian's mouth went agape. He wrinkled his brow and frowned, but lowered the gun slightly.

"I didn't know you had a lover, Mary, and especially not here in Rome. Why have you not said anything about him... or is it her?"

"Well, our relationship is a private matter. It has also been a long distance liaison for about a year now. He is the reason I wanted to come with you to Rome... I wanted to see him."

Max squinted his eyes, nodded, and said harshly as he pointed the gun at her again, "Okay, call him now!"

Mary nodded her head and dialed Faisal's cell number, setting the plan in her mind as she dialed.

"Hello."

"Yes, John, this is Mary again. Please tell the person on the phone that you are my special friend."

Maximilian rudely grabbed the phone before she could say anything else.

"How long have you been involved with Mary, John?"

There was a short pause. "Ah, it seems like a lifetime, but perhaps only for a year or so. Who is this and why do you ask?"

Maximilian frowned and handed the phone back to Mary. Mary said a few things to Faisal, then hung up the phone. She looked at Max.

Max frowned, nodded, and left the room. Mary exhaled as she sat on the bed.

∞

In Dr. Romano's cottage, Sarah looked out the window and stretched her tired body. It was getting cold and dark outside and the wind was howling down the mountain like a band of angry hyenas. She had tried over a week ago to get ahold of her brother, David, to tell him that she was all right. She figured he had heard about her being at the Vatican and the attempted murder. However, the cell phone that he had a few months ago was out of service.

She had finally and reluctantly contacted Andrew a few

days ago to tell him she was okay and for him to call her folks and David to tell them she was well. She told Andrew that she had lost their new phone numbers. He had asked where she was with such determination that she told him it would be better if he didn't know, that way they would both be safe. He went too far and said he couldn't understand that type of insanity and that he felt she didn't trust him. She had felt such an extreme chill caused by that comment that she had hung up immediately. She then quietly cried.

She now knew that it had to have been Andrew who told someone about her going to Rome. When she thought about it again, she let out a sorrowful sigh and tears ran down her cheeks. Father Dan came to her side and put his arm around her shoulder. She looked at him with tearful eyes and cried quietly on his shoulder. Alfonso and Lena watched sadly.

"Do not cry, my pet!" Lena said as she took Sarah to the kitchen to get a cup of tea and dry her tears.

Sarah confided in Lena what she thought had happened with Andrew.

"How could he hurt me like that? Why would he do that to me, Lena?" Sarah whispered.

Chapter Nine
A Voice from the Past

In the Vatican, Cardinal Giovanni Giotto answered what he assumed was his secure phone. He thought that there were only three people who knew the secret number. One was the pope, and the others were his elderly mother and another cardinal and close friend. No one else even knew the line existed. He figured since he had just heard from his 92-year-old mother this morning, it had to be the pope.

"Cardinal Giotto?" the voice asked.

"Yes, who is this?" he asked tentatively, not familiar with the voice but knowing it was not the pope.

"A person from the past, Cardinal Giovanni. It is your nephew. Is this a secure line? Can anyone tap into what we are saying?"

There was a long pause and then the cardinal, somewhat out of breath due to the shock, muttered, "No, this is a special line, no one can tap into our conversation." He paused, caught his breath again, and whispered, "We thought you were dead. I kept the press article on the horrible plane crash in the Himalayas. It was reported in the newspaper in February of last year. You and several others were described as having been killed instantly in the crash. I called Susan; she was in a terrible state. I left Rome to be with her and stayed with her for two weeks. I officiated at your funeral. My God, how could you do such a terrible thing to your own daughter?"

"Like one person once said, 'My death was highly overrated.'" After regretting what he had said, he softened his tone. "I am so very sorry, Uncle Giovanni. Sometimes we have to do things we do not wish to do."

"Yes, I see… no, that is a falsehood. I do not see, nor do I understand. One always has a choice in every situation, no matter how dire. One has a moral obligation to oneself and to God to always do what is right. Sometimes the result can be dreadful, but the correct moral choice is always the right one."

The cardinal then stopped and wrinkled his brow. "Do you still have that red birth blemish that resembles our blessed Mary on your right shoulder?"

"No, my dear uncle. I do, however, have a purple birth blemish that some say resembles Christ on my left shoulder." He paused and then said, "I take it that question was necessary?"

"Under the present circumstances, very much so. Why didn't you tell us that you were alive? How could you have done this to us, and especially to Susan? We went through agony over your death and Susan suffered terribly. You should have trusted us to keep your secret. It was terribly unfair and cruel."

"I know, Uncle Giovanni! I am well aware of all of that, believe me! I have gone through pangs of hell over it. I wanted to tell you both, but my superiors wouldn't hear of it."

The cardinal interrupted and asked, "Who could be so important that you obeyed them in such a dishonorable lie?"

"The President of the United States, Uncle Giovanni. He said no one was to ever know that I was still alive. The safety of the nation hung in the balance at the time, and by the way, it still does. I was assigned the directorship of a deeply hidden covert department that is not controlled by any division of Homeland Security; not even the Pentagon knows we exist. Only the old director of the CIA who died several months after the plan was initiated was involved in the decision; in fact, it was his idea. Once the invisible department was established, the president himself immediately destroyed all documentation and, as of that moment, we ceased to exist.

"The black agency is now totally independent of everyone in the government except the president; not even the vice president knows of our existence. I couldn't tell my own daughter, and that was even tougher than not telling you, Uncle Giovanni. I suffered unbearably when she died in an automobile accident this past June never knowing her father was still alive. I have suffered with the fact that I never got to see her again. I wasn't even allowed to go to her funeral incognito. I lost it on that occasion. I drank heavily and was incoherent for a week straight. I was lucky I was in an underground facility under the close surveillance of dedicated agents or I would have gone AWOL!

"The president called and gave his condolences and said that what I was doing was so important for America that he had to sacrifice me and my loved ones. He apologized profusely and I sobered up and started doing my job again."

"Yes, I imagine so. I officiated at Susan's funeral, as I said!" The cardinal hesitated and then said sadly, "And then there were none."

"Uncle Giovanni, I would have given anything not to have put you and Susan through all of this. I don't know what more to say... I just couldn't tell you."

"I see... and is your country safer now so you can tell me you are still alive?"

"No, my dear Uncle, the country is in more peril now than in the past. However, new developments have come up and I have convinced the president that I need to bring you into the picture. The Vatican is an important part of a nefarious plan and is in deadly peril as well."

Cardinal Giovanni shook his head and crossed himself.

"What do you want me to do and what is this terrible plan?"

"We are after an unpublished Nostradamus manuscript, the core of the deadly dilemma. We are also trying to find a Nubian scroll and a green amulet. If we do not find them and they end up in the wrong hands, America could be in a world war by the middle of 2015. The first part of the plan has already been initiated but has taken a setback since the perpetrators of the plot failed to get ahold of the items as originally planned."

"Oh, dear Lord... when will humanity learn that revenge and hatred ending in war is never the answer to anything? Our poor world is heavy with the pangs of war."

"Yes, I understand that fully, Uncle Giovanni; that is why we must find the manuscript to prevent such things occurring again in the near future."

"Okay. I will not say anything about this to anyone and will strive to find the manuscript. Dr. Addison is not part of the problem, is she? She is such a nice young lady."

"No, in fact she is an unknowing pawn in the immoral game and an obstacle to the malicious entities in this mess. Her life is danger because she is the fly in their potent ointment. I guess I must tell you the rest. She is the sister of one of my agents recently recruited from the ranks of the FBI. His name is David Addison, and he is already feeling the sorrow of sibling betrayal and it is affecting him. He had to bring Dr. Addison's boyfriend into the picture as well and now that relationship is in peril of dissolving. What a horrible mess we are in, Uncle Giovanni."

"Yes… secrecy, betrayal, and hidden agendas all have terrible results in our lives." The cardinal paused. "What do the prophecies say? I figure that is the crux of the problem. Do you know?"

"Yes, to some extent, but the manuscript is made to look like a deliberate forgery at first, but then will be revealed as true. It is a deadly plot. When we had it translated, the person didn't totally know what the manuscript entailed; however, we found that the prophecies were concerned with America and our allies in relationship to Middle Eastern nations who are hostile to us. The prophecies have to do with assassinations of high level Israeli officials, retaliations, and then a major war in the Middle East with Israel."

"But couldn't the president stop America from becoming involved as a participant in such a bloody conflict this time?"

"It appears he can't once order number 11490 is initiated."

"That is horrible. I am not familiar with the 11490 order."

"You are not alone, Uncle. The vast majority of American citizens are not aware of it. The order states that, under certain extreme and chaotic circumstances in America, a national emergency can be called."

"What does that entail?"

"It allows the government, with the Department of Homeland Security in charge, to take over every state in the United States."

"What? In every aspect? Including the citizens of each

state? What about the Constitution?"

"Yes, every state and every citizen in America comes under the control of Homeland Security. The order overrides the Constitution," he whispered.

"Dear God!" the cardinal stated as he exhaled heavily. "From what I have learned from Bishop Bindello, no one really knew what was in the new prophecies; not Dr. Addison or anyone else. How did you know about them?"

Don hesitated.

"Well, when one of our agents got ahold of the manuscript for a short time and copied it, we translated the writings to the best of our ability. However, the predictions were uncertain due to the complexity of the writings and our imprecise translations. We kept it in our safe at our underground facility for a short time so that we could continue our translation and decoding when we found an expert. However, one night before we got back with the Nostradamus expert, a deeply embedded mole in the office of Homeland Security must have become aware it was in the vault. Unfortunately, the safe was shared with a small top-secret communication group from Homeland Security sent to work with us temporarily on a decoding problem. The person stole the manuscript from the secure safe. It was at that time that it appeared to us that the Archeology Archives Corporation was also involved in the conspiracy. However, they are so entrenched with the DoD that we can't get the authorization to interfere with them at this time.

"The corporation is not only involved in the conspiracy, but may be mixed up in unethical and illegal activities in regard to artifacts. Anyway, that is why we need to find the manuscript as soon as possible. I cannot tell you any more; that would jeopardize our operation and the outcome would then be uncertain. We are trying to retrieve the Nostradamus manuscript along with a green amulet that we believe one of the parties stole from the Giza Pyramid, as well as an authentic Nubian scroll stolen from an Egyptian museum. They were hidden near a Nubian pyramid so that the excavation group from the Archeology Archives Corporation would find them and bring them out of Egypt legally. Unfortunately, or fortunately, Dr. Addison and Dr. Vachon found them before we could get someone in to collect the manuscript and destroy it. Dr. Addison, for some unknown reason, must have felt something was wrong and didn't tell the other members of her team about her find. Anyway, she absconded with the items and the distasteful process started, which put her life in immediate peril."

"Yes, I see… well, I really don't totally understand, but I do understand the seriousness of the predicament. I am glad you are alive and I will help in any way I can. I have already pressed poor Bishop Bindello to find the manuscript, but that was to make sure the Vatican gained some jurisdiction over it. Now that I know the other side of the story, I will make sure you get it first."

"Thank you, Uncle Giovanni; that is a great relief to me."

"Nothing like a good confession, is there?" He laughed slightly. "By the way, I do absolve you of your sins."

The two talked for another few minutes and then hung up their phones. Cardinal Giotto shook his head and got on his knees to pray; he failed to hear the *click* as someone in the pope's bedroom hung up a phone.

After being nosey and answering the pope's private line, accidentally overhearing the conversation, Brother Simon Defoe smiled an evil smile and left the pope's bedroom. He had originally gone there to steal some gold items from the pope's locked drawer. When he left, he went to his quarters, and from there, he made a call.

"Yes, this is Simon. I have some information that is worth a lot of money. I overheard Cardinal Giotto and another person talking about manuscripts, amulets, scrolls, and conspiracies and that his secret group worked for someone very important in the government. He said he was trying to get back a Nostradamus manuscript and asked for the cardinal's help. There were also other extremely tasty items of even more critical importance to you."

Darren Williams finally composed himself after he heard what Simon had said.

"How much do you want, Brother Simon, for the

information and your permanent silence?"

The brother said immediately, "$100,000, not one cent less."

Darren paused and, knowing that Brother Simon never charged him more than any data was worth (the only moral part of his whole being), he said, "Done! Now tell me about what you overheard!"

"Not so fast, Mr. Williams. I want the money first this time. The information is so critical it could result in many deaths, including mine. When I have the money, I will be able to escape from this lustrous prison with its lavish display of opulence and pious bastards in which I have been enslaved. I can ensure no one will know where I have gone."

There was a pause again and then Darren sighed.

"Okay, I will send the money immediately to you at the Vatican."

"No, no, I want you to transfer it to a friend of mine!"

"Yes, yes, fine. What is the account number?"

Brother Simon gave him the number and said he would write everything down that he had overheard and fax it to him just as soon as he had the money. Darren said that would be acceptable, gave him a secret fax number, and hung up the phone. He then made a phone call to make sure that Brother Simon would be going nowhere after the data arrived, nor would the spy in his midst.

Chapter Ten
The Devil Does His Work

It was a day after Darren had paid Brother Simon for the information that Brother Simon was killed in an automobile accident late at night as he was leaving the Vatican with a satchel. He did not have the satchel or any money on him when he was found.

Darren, Ralph, and Jon were sitting in Darren's hotel room in Rome later that same day. He took a bottle of 100-year-old scotch from his suitcase and poured himself and each of the others scotch and sodas in cut glass goblets that had been sitting on an antique 15th century English sideboard.

"What is the reason for the celebration, Darren? It must be important for you to dig out your most expensive scotch," Jon said as he took a sip of the smooth drink.

"Some very important information was received by fax yesterday. It will aid us in getting back the manuscript and explains why our plans have been known."

"That's wonderful news, Darren!" Ralph said as he took a sip of his drink.

"Yes it is, Ralph; it explains a lot. I also found out there is a mole in our little organization."

Jon stared at Darren.

"There are only the three of us and the corporation executives. Who is it?"

"Ralph, would you like to explain who that could be?" Darren said as he glared at Ralph.

Ralph's eyes widened and he got up to leave but then clutched at his throat.

"You… you poisoned me, you insane idiot!" He toppled over onto the floor as Jon watched in horror and Darren laughed.

"How could you do that, Darren? What is going on here?" Jon asked incredulously as he stared at the still body of Ralph lying askew on an oriental rug.

"I was just informed by a perfectly reliable source that

there was a spy in our midst, and I knew immediately due to the specificity of the information that it had to be Ralph. He is in with some top-secret group. He had informed his group that we forged the Nostradamus manuscript and stole it from a safe at a secret underground facility. They knew that what we wrote predicted a threat to the peace in the Middle East and required that the United States go to war. He also alerted his group about the items stolen from the Egyptian museum and the Giza Pyramid, and that we buried all of the items in the Nubian area along with our forged manuscript. He also informed them that the Archeology Archives Corporation was given a no-bid contract procured by us to find and send the items back."

Jon sat back in his chair, stunned.

"Who was it that told you about all of this?"

"My ex mole, he is now dead. He said he never heard the person's name, only that he was in charge of a black agency that is entirely independent of everyone in the government except the president. Not even the vice president knows of the organization's existence. I also found out that Dr. Addison's brother is a CIA operative in the organization."

"My god, they must be the other ones that we encountered while looking for Dr. Addison!"

"Yes, I think you're right, Jon. Anyway, it seems it was just a bad piece of luck that Dr. Addison and Dr. Vachon found the items before our people could get to them. Ralph must have been the one that alerted David Addison about our CIA agents and the security personnel from the Archeology Archives Corporation. I would guess that he kept Addison and his group informed of our progress. It could have been worse! If one of my people hadn't heard the CIA personnel talking about our stolen manuscript when it was put in the safe at the underground facility, we would have been out of luck!"

"That had to have been right after we first had the manuscript forged."

"Yes. Ralph had to have been the one who stole it from us originally. That traitor almost ruined our plan in the beginning. It was lucky we were able to steal it back in a short time."

Darren called in two agents and had them roll Ralph's body up in a rug and take him away to a warehouse in an underground facility to be disposed of later. Jon was still stunned with disbelief.

"Darren, are you sure about all of this?"

"Yes. After getting the information from my mole this morning, I called someone. He said he believed David Addison had hired Ralph. I put two and two together and figured Addison put Ralph in with us because he thought we were involved in the plot! It could only be him or you, Jon. It wasn't you, was it, Jon?"

"Good god no, Darren! That means a covert CIA group knows all about us, the Nostradamus manuscript, and our plan! What are we going to do now?" Jon asked nervously. "And why would David Addison tell all of that to one of ours?"

Darren didn't answer the question but said, "When we get the manuscript back and all hell breaks loose, we will have our comrades in Homeland Security determine who the agents are and dispose of them. Remember, we will have order 11490 in full authority at that time. Don't worry!" Darren laughed.

"Don't they know the people in the group that was with them in the underground facility?"

"Unfortunately, two people in the group have disappeared and the one who stole the manuscript back for us died shortly after he got it."

Jon looked at Darren and nodded but didn't drink any more of his scotch and soda.

∞

While all of this was taking place, David approached the door of Professor Romano's cottage. He took a deep breath and used the bronze iron knocker.

Sarah looked at Alfonso.

"Who could that be, Alfonso? We haven't heard from anyone in weeks…."

"I am not sure, Sarah, but don't worry; I will get rid of them. I'll tell them Lena has a bad cold."

When Alfonso opened the door, David and Olaf pushed their way in and closed the door before Alfonso could react. Sarah gasped and ran over to her brother, pointing a finger in his face.

"David, what are you doing here? How did you know I was here?"

"Dear little sister of mine, don't you give me that red-haired, angry stare. I have been trying to find you for weeks now. I have been worried to death about you! I finally discovered your whereabouts after you called Andrew."

"But I didn't tell that traitor where I was!" Sara fumed. "He was the one who told the others that I was in Rome, too, wasn't he?"

"No, Sarah. Andrew told me after you left with Father Dan. He didn't tell anyone else. The second time, after he said he wasn't going to help me anymore, we tapped into his phone. When you called him the second time and asked him to tell us that you were okay, we triangulated the phone from which you called. It was easy to locate the address after that."

"Are you and Andrew part of this terrible scheme? Oh god, I couldn't stand *two* people betraying me! What do you want?"

"Sarah, please sit down and I will tell you the whole story. But first, Andrew is not a traitor and neither am I. He was helping me so that I could help you! I am with the CIA now, on special assignment from my FBI job."

After Sarah gained her composure and everyone was introduced, the group sat down and listened as he told his story. After he got through, Alfonso got up, stretched, and glanced out the front window.

Dusk was starting to cover the hillside with a shadowy blanket. He saw umbrae mulling across the street a few blocks away. He then went to a side window and saw some people down a block on the other side of the street. He told David.

David took out his gun and told the others to hide in the bedroom. Just as he reached the back porch, the door flung open and a hooded man with another man, both holding identical crossbows, stood in front of him.

The man said, "Mr. Addison, please put your gun down. We are not here to harm you or your sister; we are here to help you. Faisal saved the life of Dr. Vachon at Keller's Knoll and Dr. Addison at the Vatican. Some covert CIA agents and a group from a private security firm as well as the security personnel from the corporation just arrived nearby. They are checking out every house in the area. They located the general area where they thought Dr. Addison might be. They are up a few blocks and across the street now but will be here soon. Please get Sarah, the manuscript, scroll, and amulet and come with us. Please, do not hesitate or I am afraid there will be bloodshed; the others are here to kill you and everyone else involved!"

David hesitated for just a moment, looked into the black man's eyes, put his gun in his holster, and went to get his sister. He asked her to come with him and told the others to leave the cottage from the back door and go to a friend's house for the time being.

A few blocks from the cottage, Jon Pierce spoke on the phone to Irina, the two covert CIA agents, and the five new private security agents.

"We have searched all of the houses in the area except the two houses down the block and across the street. Irina, take Thomas and Ford with you and search the house to the right, Peters and Samson and the rest of you search the house next to it. If any of you find Dr. Addison, call me immediately."

David and Sarah ran out of the back of the house with the two black men and the others ran to a house far down the hill. They had only been gone a few minutes when Irina, Thomas, and Ford went into the Romanos' cottage with guns raised.

"There is no one in the living room. Go to the other rooms and see if there is any trace that Dr. Addison has been here," Irina stated.

After a thorough search, they left and Irina called Jon.

"We have nothing here," she said. "How about Peters and Samson?"

"Damn!" Jon cursed. "No, they just found a widow who

is hard of hearing and almost blind. She said she saw nothing and heard nothing! Of course, in her case, it seems plausible." He cursed and made another call.

"Yes?"

"Darren, Jon here. Dr. Addison was not in any of the houses in the area where we thought she was. They must have known we were coming if they were even there in the first place."

Darren sighed and thought about the situation. It had to be one of the corporation's people who alerted Dr. Addison.

"Jon, keep looking for her!" He frowned, hung up the phone, and then made another call.

∞

"Yeah, this is Maximilian."

"Max, Darren here. We found a mole in our group here! It was Ralph…. Yes, I got the information from a once reliable informer. Unfortunately, he is no longer with us. … What? I mean he is no longer among the living. … Anyway, he said there was a mole in your group as well. At first, I figured it might have been someone in Homeland Security who overheard our man, but as I think about it now, I don't see that as a possibility. Do you suspect anyone?"

Maximilian thought back about Mary's conversation that he had overheard.

"Damn, I was tricked! Yes, I think I know who it is." With that, he hung up the phone with a bang.

He ran to Mary's bedroom with his gun drawn, but she was gone. A note was left on the bed.

Dear Max, you are a stupid brute! Do you really think that Darren is going to let you and the rest of your greedy little group go free? I know for a fact if the manuscript is found and the fireworks start, all of you are dead. It was signed Mary 'Mona' Drew.

Maximilian cursed and called Daniel Smyth.

"Daniel, we have problems."

"Yes, I know. We still haven't found Dr. Addison or the

manuscript. Jon called and said they came up empty-handed after searching the area they thought she would be."

"No, I mean another problem. Mary Drew was a spy for someone."

"What? Who?"

"I don't know for sure; she probably works for some government agency. Everything we have been doing and saying about our plans, she has probably related to her group. She also put something in my mind that had been fermenting there for some time now, Daniel. She said if the manuscript is found and the plan is initiated, Darren will have all of us killed."

"We have to get the hell out of here, Max. Did Johanna get everything ready to destroy our computer data?"

"Yes, I will call her immediately and I'll get our corporation jet ready right away. Contact Horace and David, I will contact Derek, Dr. Sato, and Johanna."

"What about Irina?"

"She is on her own now."

"Okay, Max."

Mary Drew smiled as she listened in on the conversation from a van near the corporation's headquarters. She had tapped the phone before she left. She made a call to Dr. Don Gamble.

"Dr. Gamble, the corporation executives are scuttling the ship.... Yes, they are calling everyone and will meet at a private airport just outside of San Francisco where their jet is based." She told him which airport.

"Wonderful news, Mary! I will get some CIA agents to meet them there. When they all arrive, we can arrest them."

"How are David and Olaf doing in their search for Dr. Addison?"

"They located her in a cottage in Rome. The problem is that the two covert CIA men, Irina, and some new private security agents narrowed down the location. Oh, I have some bad news, too. David's mole, a man named Ralph, was found out as being a mole. I didn't know he had hired Ralph."

"I thought you knew about Ralph."

"No, I just found out. Anyway, I don't know what

happened to him; at this time, all communications have been quiet. He may have been killed."

"I can't believe Ralph may be dead. Do we have any idea where Darren is now?"

"No, he disappeared as well and we think he flew out of Rome on his private jet, possibly to California. After he found out about Ralph being a mole, he went underground. He has had no communications with anyone, not even Jon, who is still running the show in Rome.

∞

While the corporation executives scrambled to get to their private Learjet and fly to the islands near Haiti, Darren was almost in Santa Rosa, California. Sarah, David, and Olaf were in a cab heading to a small private military airport on the outskirts of Rome and the two Nubians were with them.

"David, what is your part in this scheme?" Sarah asked, somewhat confused.

"I am part of a legitimate covert CIA group that is trying to locate the manuscript."

"What? Oh, David, not you, too!" Sarah whispered.

"It's not what you think; our group works directly for the President of the United States. We're trying to stop the manuscript from being aired by the conspirators so they can't initiate their plans. We had plans to destroy it, but you found it first."

"But David, the manuscript is a forgery."

"We are aware of that, Sarah… it was forged to convince the populace and congress to believe in the new prophecies. The first prophecy has to do with the assassination of a high-ranking Israeli statesman. It foreshadows the rest that will happen according to the prophecies. In other words, they will say that since it predicted the assassination, the other prophecies have to be accurate as well. They will also have the scroll and amulet to authenticate the manuscript."

"That is what we translated, too. But David, how could

they know about any assassination?"

"Easy, they will be part of the assassination plot!"

"Oh, my god, can they be *that* horrible? Do they have no souls, no sense of justice or mercy?"

"I am afraid so. Like the elephant man said, 'If this be your justice, I would hate to see your mercy,' or something like that."

The Nubians nodded and looked out the plane's windows. They still had their qualms about the US government's involvement with the manuscript, scroll, and amulet.

Olaf piloted the small jet out over the ocean, and as the airplane droned on and Sarah and the Nubians fell asleep, David made a call.

"Yes."

"David here. I have Sarah and the manuscript. She and the others are asleep now," he whispered.

"Thank God you got her and the manuscript! I take it she believed you?"

"Of course, why wouldn't she? I'm her brother," David said and laughed quietly. "By the way, I have two Nubian men aboard. They saved our skins at the Romano cottage. The tall man was the one who shot both Yide and Omar in the shoulder to keep them from shooting Dr. Vachon and Sarah."

There was a long pause before Dr. Gamble said, "It was not a good idea to allow them to get on board, David. Watch them closely. Have Olaf fly to our Santa Rosa facility at 38 degrees 26.4 minutes north and 122 degrees and 42.9 minutes west. I will meet you there in about 14 hours. By the way, we took care of the corporation executives."

David repeated the coordinates and gave them to Olaf. He nodded and adjusted the plane's direction.

David came back, sat down, and continued his conversation with Dr. Gamble.

"It seems things are finally going our way now, Don. The only ones we have to take care of now we can count on our fingers. I'll see you in about 13 hours. I am going to get some sleep now, too." David hung up the phone and thought that it was odd of Don to say the executives were taken care of instead of being arrested, but he didn't give it another thought.

Sarah blinked and tried not to make a noise. She didn't want David to know that she had overheard everything. She shivered and felt a cold current of air drift over her body like a gust of wind from an icy pond. She didn't know what to think of the conversation. She didn't want to suspect her brother of foul play, but she didn't like the sound of what she had heard. She peeked over at the Nubian men. The one called Faisal, who had saved her life, appeared to be sound asleep, as did his partner.

She quietly opened her cell phone and made a call to Father Dan. She whispered quietly into her cell. She told him about the conversation she overheard including their destination in Santa Rosa. She clicked off the phone and laid her head down on the pillow. Her hands were clammy and her mind was racing; she felt trapped and impotent. She also felt angry.

Father Dan was on his way to America when he got Sarah's call. He listened and said he would try to come up with something, although he wasn't sure if what she had overheard was as nefarious as it sounded.

She told him if he had to contact her with bad news to let it ring once and hang up. That way she could call back when it was safe to talk. He agreed and told her to be safe, and that his prayers would be with her. He fidgeted in his seat and finally, after much deliberation, decided he needed to call Cardinal Giotto. He believed in the devout man with all of his heart and soul and trusted him implicitly.

Father Dan shivered and felt an icy reality starting to sink into his soul. He shook his head helplessly as the 747 droned on in the stormy heavens. He sat and looked at the dark clouds forming outside the window. He fingered his rosary beads and prayed, unable to do anything else.

Chapter Eleven
Things Are Not What They Seem

The 747 whined on and Father Dan continued to pray about the situation. He was finally able to contact Cardinal Giotto on his third try.

"I don't know what to think, Cardinal Giotto. Sarah sounded sure that her brother was part of some nefarious plot, but she didn't know what part! I have to help her somehow!"

"I can assure you, Father Dan, he is not part of the evil scheme. He is on the side of good and works for my nephew, Dr. Donald Gamble. I know my nephew would never be up to anything reprehensible. Don is a fine man and he said David was one of his agents. Perhaps Dr. Addison has had so many terrible experiences lately that she jumps to immediate and erroneous conclusions."

"Yes, yes, perhaps you are right, Cardinal. I won't worry about it for now, but I do have a concern." He paused. "I thought your nephew was killed in a plane accident a year or so ago."

"Yes, I did, too, but I got a phone call from him a short time ago and he explained the cover-up was part of some secret thing. Anyway, thanks to God, he is still alive. I understand your feelings on the other matter; it is always a good idea to have some concerns, Father Dan. I will pray for you."

"Thank you, Sir, I need it!"

When the phone call was over, Cardinal Giotto called his nephew.

"Yes."

"Don, it is Giovanni."

"Uh… yes, Uncle, how are you? Is there a problem?"

"No, Don. You said just to call you if anything came up. Well, I just got a call from Father Dan and…."

After Cardinal Giotto got through explaining the situation, there was a long pause before Don told him that everything was fine and not to be anxious. He said that Dr. Addison was worrying over nothing.

Cardinal Giotto put the phone down. He looked at the pewter cross with Jesus hanging on his wall and felt a pang of cold apprehension. For some unknown reason, he started to worry about the call he had just made. He then got on his knees and started praying. As he was praying, there was a knock on his door.

"Cardinal Giotto, it is Bishop Bindello."

"Bishop Bindello, come in! You look concerned. What is the problem, my dear friend?"

"I have been very worried ever since you told me that your nephew had called you. The one you originally thought to have been killed in the plane crash."

"Yes, yes, I see. And why is that, Adamo?"

"Well, after you told me about your nephew being alive, I felt uncomfortable for some reason that only God knows. I decided to make some calls to a few of my friends in the FAA. I am an amateur pilot, you know."

"I understand, and what did you find?"

"Uh, Cardinal Giotto, uh… I am so sorry. I learned that your nephew, Donald Gamble, actually *did* die in the plane accident."

"What? How can that be? Adamo, I listened to him; he knew about the birth mark and everything. You must be mistaken!"

"I'm afraid not, sir. A very good and close friend of his, a man named Thomas Castle, verified without a doubt that the body was that of Don Gamble. He saw the body. He had a bluish red birthmark of Christ on his shoulder, and his face was recognizable. I just got word this morning. Thomas had been out of the country ever since the accident. He is an environmentalist and was in Chile. My friend, who was in Chile with him at the time, asked him about my concerns. That was after I called him about your nephew. My friend called me this morning with the information. I hadn't had the opportunity to tell you since you were in meetings all morning."

"My dear God, how could that be true? I talked to him! I was so sure!"

"Yes, I know you talked to someone, Sir, but you didn't *see* your nephew, did you?"

The cardinal paused and shook his head.

"My God, who could it have been, then? Are this imposter and David Addison involved in something evil? Oh, dear Lord, what do we do now? I just made a phone call and told who I thought to be Don everything that Father Dan had told me. If my nephew is dead, then the man I thought was my nephew must be part of the nefarious plot and Sarah is in deep peril! Perhaps her brother is part of the plot, too! Oh, dear God!"

"I don't know, Sir… perhaps David Addison was fooled, too!"

"You have to get ahold of Sarah immediately and warn her."

"Yes, I will, Cardinal."

Bishop Bindello left and went to his room. He shook his head anxiously and made the call. Father Dan listened intently then wrinkled his brow and shook his head sadly. He thanked the bishop and called Sarah. He let the phone ring just once and hung up. Sarah had her cell on vibrate and, feeling just one pulsation, she knew that Father Dan had called, meaning something was terribly wrong.

She looked at the two Nubian men who seemed to be sleeping peacefully and made a muted call to Father Dan. They talked for about two minutes. When she hung up, her heart was pounding rapidly and she was trembling. She gathered herself back together as much as possible and looked at the two silent black men, wondering if she could trust them. David still hadn't come back from the cockpit, and she had the perfect opportunity to talk to them in private. She felt she had no choice but to confide in them and went over to where they were sleeping.

Faisal awoke and looked at Sarah, who was visibly trembling as she stared at his face.

"Dearest lady, your distressing eyes betray the dismay hidden in your heart. Your thoughts appear to have gone to some dark and ghostly field where lies and treachery live, and their piercing thrusts and bloody stabs have been inflicted upon your innocent mind. A fading shadow lingers across your countenance and the dark red of your hair that falls upon your worried brow is lit by the sun's angry glare. You appear drowned in beads of hopelessness and anxiety. My dear child, what have you learned that is so hideous?"

After telling the two Nubians about the problem, the men nodded their heads and one of them took her hand in his.

"I am sure David is not an evil man, Dr. Addison. I have felt the rhythms of his soul and know he is good. Perhaps, however, from what you have heard, his superior is not what he seems. I believe that your brother may have been deceived as well. We will keep our promise to protect you. Do not fear!"

"Faisal, please take the Nubian scroll and the amulet; they belong to your people. If something happens, you must escape with them."

Faisal smiled, took the items, and put them in a hidden pocket on the inside of his robe.

"Thank you, Dr. Addison. Kashta will be very pleased the items have been returned. They are of sacred importance to us."

David came back and looked at the three talking. He hesitated as he looked back and forth between them and then spoke.

"We will be landing in about eight hours. You should all try to get some more sleep before we land. I know I am."

Sarah longed to ask David about the true nature of his search for the manuscript but didn't want the cold disappointment of what he might reveal. She couldn't stand it if he was part of a dark and evil conspiracy. She fell into a deep, disturbed sleep that contained nightmarish images.

In her traumatic dream, she witnessed herself looking into a hazy mirror that had a dark image. A reflection of a dismal thing down a black chasm reached her wild eyes. The wretched thing held a silent scream on its lips and stared back at her with eyes that were covered with scabs of black. She looked closer at the pitiful face and saw that it was an exhausted vagabond with blurry, hopeless eyes. Then the image cleared and she saw it was herself. She screamed inside her mind and the scene changed. An artist who was painting her image looked through her and saw the fear that gripped her soul. In ashen surprise, he whispered as he looked to a cross on the wall. 'How am I to paint such a pitiful child?' A muted voice that echoed from the heavenly firmament said to him, 'Not the poor wretched waif you see before you, for the piteous image still and silent is only a deceptive disguise made up of terrible moments and the dust of terror that clings to her.' The artist sobbed, then looked again and saw the bleak image fade and a beautiful figure sat before him, shimmering in the sun. He painted a brilliant halo over her head and allowed the sun to warm the image. It became one of hope and redemption.

Sarah awoke and sighed. The plane droned on as David and the two other men slept.

Olaf turned up the radio and heard the news that a corporation jet holding executives from the Archeology Archives Corporation had been found in the mountains of Marquesas Island. It was reported that it had been scheduled for a private airport somewhere in the Tuamotu Islands. All those aboard the plane had been killed instantly upon impact. They said the reason for the crash was being investigated. It appeared that some people on the island heard an explosion before the plane nosed toward earth; they said they saw the jet blow apart mid-air prior to crashing.

Olaf called to David, who awoke and went to the cabin.

"What is it, Olaf?" he said sleepily.

"I just heard over the radio that the executives from the Archeology Archives Corporation were all killed in a plane crash. It was reported that there was an explosion aboard before the plane crashed into the side of the mountain."

"What, where was that?"

"In the mountains of Marquesas Island."

"My god, that can't be… Don said he had taken care of them. How did they escape from the authorities?"

"I have no idea, David, but the crash is believed to have been caused under highly suspicious circumstances. There was no word by the TV news anchor or any indication from anyone that they were escapees or had even been arrested by anyone."

David shivered, shook his head, and went back to the other part of the plane where the others were still asleep. He started to go to sleep when his cell phone rang; he answered it immediately so he wouldn't disturb the others.

"Yes, this is David."

"David Addison?"

"Yes, and who is this?"

"This is Father Dan Murphy. We met at Professor Romano's cottage in Rome."

"Oh yes, Father, I am glad you are safe. What can I do for you?"

"This is a very delicate matter and I am putting my faith in God and in the fact that I sense you are a good and honest man. I am putting the life of your sister in your hands, and I pray that what I am doing is right!"

David wrinkled his brow and paused as the drone of the jet filled the air with an eerie silence.

"I don't understand, Father. Is there something you wish to say?"

"You do love your sister, don't you? And you wouldn't think of ever harming her?"

"Of course, Father, why would you ask such a thing? I love my sister; we are a very close family. I would never think of harming her!"

"Then I will believe you, and may God strike me dead if I am wrong. Let me give you some information which I feel may be very upsetting to you."

David listened to the story about Dr. Don Gamble and Cardinal Giotto. He then thought about what Don had said about the corporation executives, that they had been taken care of. He put that together with the crash and what Father Dan had told him and he put his head in his hands. He muttered out loud.

"Oh, my god, what have I been involved in? What have I done?"

Sarah woke in time to hear him moan.

"David, what's wrong?"

He told her the whole story. Sarah then confessed that she

had heard the same thing from Father Dan and didn't know what to say or if she could trust him.

"Sarah, how could you believe that I would ever lie to you or allow any harm come to you?"

"I am sorry, David.... I am so sorry."

One of the black men who David thought was asleep placed a hand on his arm.

"We knew that there was a spy in your midst, but we didn't know who it was. We thought perhaps it was you for a while, but decided that you were not the evil one. We came to the same conclusion about Olaf before we found out that one of those involved in the Nostradamus scheme from the beginning, perhaps even the instigator of the conspiracy, was a high level person in Homeland Security. At first we only knew of Dr. Gamble as a top CIA operative who was killed in a crash. When we heard what he had said to Cardinal Giotto, we wondered if it was really him. Our superior obtained pictures of him. While being your superior, did he always have his face wrapped in bandages?"

"Yes, he said that after the plane accident, he had to have plastic surgery. He said he was still healing and would have his face covered for about another month."

"Yes, that all makes sense. We then were told by Sarah that she had learned from Father Dan that there was verifiable confirmation that the real Dr. Don Gamble was in fact killed in a plane crash."

"Yes, Father Dan just called me and told me all of that, too. I had not heard anything about the death of Dr. Gamble being verified until Father Dan just called."

"Was his face bandaged the whole time after you were recruited?"

"Yes, same with Olaf who was recruited from MI6. Both of us have only seen him with his face bandaged."

"Then Father Dan is probably correct… your superior is not Dr. Gamble."

"Oh, David, I am so sorry! What do we do now?" Sarah asked sadly.

"I need to tell Olaf and then we need to design a plan. I

am sure Dr. Gamble, or whoever he is, has people waiting for us at the private airport in Santa Rosa or in the underground base. If we show any sign that we know, we will be killed immediately! He probably plans to kill us anyway after he obtains the manuscript."

Faisal looked at David.

"You have the two of us as well, David, and I will call Leila and Mona; they are experts in the crossbow, too. The two are in San Francisco now. I will tell them the coordinates of the underground base; they will be there before we land. Perhaps another may be of help, too. We informed Ralph Anderson of the possibility of an attempt on his life by Darren Williams. I hope that he was able to do something so he wasn't murdered."

"My god, do you think Ralph is still alive? He worked under me as a mole to spy on Darren Williams and Jon Pierce, as you are probably aware. I had no idea his life was in jeopardy. I should have known when he didn't call me as often as he did in the past that something was wrong. Neither Darren or Don, or whoever he is, knew about Ralph. I personally recruited him. Gamble said to get who I wanted to get the job done. I didn't bother to tell him about Ralph until just a few days ago."

"That was probably very fortunate, David, you probably wouldn't have gotten a lot of the information you did if Gamble had known from the beginning. Ralph would have had an unfortunate accident a long time ago."

David nodded, thanked them, and went in to tell Olaf the bad news. Faisal called Mona to tell her of the problem.

After telling Olaf about Gamble, David sat with him for some time, discussing the problem. Finally, he went back to the other area and sat down with Sarah.

"I am so sorry, sis. This is not where you ought to be. Olaf and I have devised a plan. If you get the opportunity when we land, try to escape with the manuscript."

"No, David; that would alert him to the fact that we know about his involvement. He would kill you right away! We must stop him and only surprise will do it. He probably doesn't realize that we know about him. We have to act as if we know nothing about him being one of the conspirators. That is the only way we will be able to overcome him in the immediate future."

The drone of the airplane blew wafts of terrifying sounds tangled with anxious shadows across the four perplexed souls who sat in silence. Each person was in his or her own world. Sarah was sick with worry. The Nubians were worn and weary from their constant struggles combating malevolent and greedy people. As the darkening clouds plunged slowly into the western horizon underneath the skies of pink and orange, the terrible apparitions below were hidden from earth and sky. The painted clouds covered the dusky evening and the air teemed with the iciness of frozen lies kept hidden from those who search for justice and morality. The earth was entombed by the chillness of those with immorality in their souls, and who only searched for wealth and power.

Sarah looked out the window to the pale yellow lights of the city of Santa Rosa and shuddered. She looked at Faisal and he smiled; she smiled back hesitantly.

"Do not worry, Sarah. We shall prevail. Our sense of justice, like yours, is the same as all honorable people in the world. In the end, we shall win the battle alongside those who strive for integrity and morality, and who attempt to dwell with honor on this tiny bit of soil called Earth."

David looked up as the plane made a turn toward a private airport hidden in the darkness below. He went to sit in the cockpit with Olaf as they went over their final plans, neither one sure of the outcome.

∞

Below, in the depths of the underground base, several men sat together. Jon Pierce looked somber. The man who said he was Don Gamble, with his face no longer covered with bandages, sat at his desk thumping the top with a pencil and nervous energy.

"Did you have to kill *all* of the Archeology Archives Corporation executives, Philip? Wasn't there another way?" Jon asked somberly.

The Assistant Director of FEMA Philip Lodge, known erroneously to those in the small covert CIA group as Dr. Don Gamble, nodded nonchalantly.

"It was the most expedient way, Jon. We must not dwell on the few casualties it takes to forge our dreams. What is important is that we succeed, regardless of the casualties. Remember, the gaining of personal wealth and power is never evil."

Darren said, "Blowing the hell out of all the Archeology Archives Corporation executives was necessary, Jon, they were a tremendous liability. They would have thwarted our plan just to sell the manuscript and line their pockets with our money. It was a righteous call."

"Well, what do we do now? David and Olaf do not know about you, Philip, but they will eventually know something is amiss. Do we murder all of them as well?" Jon asked, not wanting to hear the answer.

Philip smiled and nodded his head.

"Jon, Jon, why the sudden desire to be so damn snowy white? You have been a part of this from the start and you know we must kill all of them; we have no choice. What is the problem?"

"Nothing... I just don't like the murdering of innocents," he said sadly.

"You didn't have a problem helping to plan the assassination of an Israeli statesman. You didn't put up a fuss with the idea of the future killing of hundreds of thousands of Arabs and Jews in our planned war. You didn't kick up your dander when we discussed the riots with hundreds of thousands of Muslims where you knew damn well that tens of thousands would probably die. You didn't even let out a peep when we discussed the use of super bombs on the Middle Eastern nations in order to take over their oil. When did you find your scruples or your stupid, petty principles?"

"I guess I'm just tired, Philip. I think I need some sleep."

"Yes, you go do that, Jon. We will talk later."

When Jon left, Philip spoke to agent Thomas.

"We have a security breach, Agent Thomas. I found out that Jon is a traitor. Please make sure he does not wake up from his nap."

Thomas nodded, took about four men with him, and headed out of the office.

"Well, Darren, it looks like it's just you and me."

"Yes, and our generals at the Pentagon and our conservative congressmen and senators who are part of our grand plan. By the way, General Davis, Peters, and Hallstead were very pleased with the way you handled the treasonous executives from the corporation."

"Yes, well I told them they were all progressive Democrats who planned to lobby the legislators to remove billions of dollars from the Department of Defense!" He laughed. "Actually I told them they were going to contact the media with the knowledge of the Nostradamus manuscript, which would have ruined our mutually beneficial scheme."

"What are we going to do with David Addison and the rest?"

"As I told Jon, we will have to kill them. But first, we will need to determine who else knows about the manuscript. We cannot have anyone, not even the religious at the Vatican, telling the truth about our forgery. However, I don't see any need to kill the religious at the Vatican at this time."

"Why doesn't it make any difference if the religious say anything?" Jon asked.

"Who believes the crazy mystic Catholics in the Vatican in Rome? The church there is not trusted after all of the troubles they have had. If they say anything about a Nostradamus manuscript, it will be dismissed as stupid, mystical ravings. Besides, they are so closed-mouth they would never say a word to the outside until it is too late, anyway."

∞

As the plane circled to make a landing, David was talking to the two Nubians.

"Unfortunately, when we first got on board I told Don or whoever he is that you two were on board, so there is no way we can sneak you off."

"Do not worry, David; we never thought of sneaking off. Besides, since they do not know that we are aware of their scheme, we are at a great advantage. We wouldn't leave you and Sarah at their mercies for any reason, anyway," Faisal stated.

"You and your partner seem to have quiet souls. You never appear to get nervous or anxious, even in the face of possible death. What keeps you that way?"

Faisal nodded, smiled, and said, "When you understand the mysteries of existence, you no longer fear death. To be born and to die are both expressions of courage!"

"I guess I am not there yet, Faisal. I still have a lot of growing to do and a lot of mysteries to solve. I will also do whatever I need to do to make that happen for all of us," David said as he checked the automatic pistol in his holster.

Sarah sat quietly vacillating between fear and anger, but knew she would act to persevere as well.

The plane started its descent to the landing field below. Olaf was nursing his ambiguous feelings. He felt the soft landing as the wheels touched gently on the tarmac and then shut off the engines. He wondered if he would ever see his wife and children again.

Chapter Twelve
And Then There Were None

The people on board tensed in nervous anticipation. Each of them had their own thoughts as to what was waiting for them below. After the plane landed, Philip had his face bandaged again and six of his private agents with AK-47's stood to the side, waiting to see what David and those on board the jet would do as they stepped off the plane.

David took a deep breath, got out hand in hand with Sarah, smiled, raised his hand in a big wave, and yelled enthusiastically.

"Don, we are very glad to be home. We have the Nostradamus manuscript, it is now safe, and so is America."

Philip smiled. His tension eased and his demeanor softened, and he told the agents to put their rifles on safety and walked over to shake David's had.

"I am glad you are here, David! And this lovely child must be your sister. Dr. Addison, I am so glad that you are safe! It has been a terrible adventure for you."

"Thank you, Dr. Gamble! I am so glad to be here, too… I'm very tired of running and being in danger. Oh, Dr. Gamble; this is Faisal and Pinaki. They are Nubians and have been my protectors."

"I am happy to meet you, too," he said, cautiously shaking their soft hands, but avoiding their black soul-piercing eyes. "Thank you for protecting David's sister, both he and I are forever grateful. Well, it appears we are finally about to end this horrible conundrum!"

"Yes, Dr. Gamble. The end and the beginning have a strange similarity in both life and death, and hope and hopelessness. May we always be able to know the difference and be on guard to overcome the power of the opposite, which is the ultimate evil."

Philip gazed at Faisal with a perplexed look and frowned slightly. He then awakened from the curious hold the eyes of the black man and his words had on him.

"Yes, yes; I understand and agree. Uh, it is time for us to go below. We have much to discuss and I am sure you are all hungry. I have a delicious dinner all prepared and waiting."

David and his group followed Philip. The six agents, with their rifles pointing to the ground, followed them. As they neared the elevator, Agents Thomas and Ford came out.

Philip said, "David, you, Olaf, and Sarah come with me and three of my agents. Agents Russell, Ford, and Thomas, Faisal, and Pianki will then come down when we send the elevator back up. We don't want to put too much of a strain on it. It was made by the lowest bidder, you know." He then laughed as he looked at the others. Everyone laughed, and Philip had no idea the laughs were faked.

When the small elevator started silently down into the black abdomen of the hidden underground base, David asked, "Don, what happened to Ralph?"

Philip jerked slightly and answered, "Uh, Ralph is downstairs waiting for us. Why do you ask?"

"I was just worried about him because I haven't heard from him for some time now. It will be good to see him."

"Yes, I see," Philip said, wondering if he had made a blunder by being tense and telling David that Ralph was there in the facility.

When the elevator reached about a quarter of a mile down, it stopped and the group got out. The elevator then started slowly back up to the top to get Faisal, Pianki, and the other agents. Don and his group walked toward a building to the east.

∞

Above the large underground facility, Faisal saw Mona, Farah, and Leila out of the corner of his eye. He nodded slightly, moved to the side, and started a conversation with agent Davidson.

"How long have you worked for Dr. Gamble and the CIA?"

Agent Ford looked at the ebony-faced man and frowned.

"For about six months. I was with White House security prior to that time. Why do you ask?"

"I was just wondering. Dr. Gamble seems to be very capable."

"Yes. However, I was recruited by the Assistant Director of Homeland Security, not Dr. Gamble."

Faisal heard the sharp twang of the bow before the others did; three of the agents went down with arrows in their shoulders. Davidson raised his AK-47 and the remaining two agents followed suit, but Faisal and Pinaki overcame them. The agents were all tied up, gagged, and hidden in bushes near the landing field.

Faisal shook his head and made a phone call.

"Sire, we have overcome the agents and will be going down into the cave of evil very shortly. Do you have any instructions?"

"Yes, Faisal, do you have the Nubian scroll and amulet?"

"Yes, Sire. Dr. Addison gave them to me before we landed."

"Very good. Please give them to Farah and have her bring them back here. If things go bad, at least we will have the precious relics. Go with Allah."

"Yes, Sire."

"And Faisal, may the Infinite Existence be with you."

"Thank you, Sire. Goodbye."

"Farah, I have the scroll and amulet in my robe; He wishes you to take them and return them to him."

"But what about all of you? I need to stay here and help!" she stated anxiously.

"No, Farah. He wishes you to go to Him with the relics. We, with the help of the Infinite Existence, will meet you back home later next week."

Farah nodded sadly, took the relics, and put them inside a satchel she was carrying that contained other documents. She nodded and headed slowly back to a car hidden a few hundred yards up from the facility behind heavy shrubbery. Faisal watched her leave, sighed, and went back to the others.

Faisal looked at Mona and Leila and said, "Thank goodness you found us. I think we now have a chance." As he said this, the elevator opened; it was empty. They got on the elevator and headed downward to the unknown, each with their own thoughts weaving through their minds.

∞

About 15 minutes prior to the incident above, three agents raised their AK-47s and disarmed David and Olaf after they got off of the elevator. They then took the Nostradamus manuscript from Sarah. Darren Williams stepped out from another room and stood beside Philip.

David looked at Dr. Gamble and asked, "Don, what is this all about? Why are you doing this?"

Darren smiled.

"Well, well, Mr. Addison... it appears that you, your feisty sister, and Olaf are in the type of trouble that one just doesn't get out of in one piece."

"I guess my little recruiting ruse with the FBI paid off very well, David. We have your sister *and* the Nostradamus manuscript now!" Dr. Gamble stated. "However, where is the amulet and scroll?"

"You greedy, despicable animals! You will never get away with this. Others know that the manuscript is a forgery now and will attest to that when you come out with your phony predictions and start your warring conflicts. The amulet and scroll are safely with someone else."

"Now, now, Olaf, don't get so upset over things. Someone has to win and someone has to lose; it's just your turn to lose," he laughed. "And about all of those who know the manuscript is a forgery, which is about three, no one will believe some weird Catholic priests in the Vatican about some wild conspiracy concerning fake Nostradamus prophecies. Those people have too many problems of their own now to be thought of as credible."

"What about the others?" Sarah asked.

"I don't think there are any others that anyone would believe, Sarah, but your little ruse was cute."

"So Dr. Gamble, or whoever you are, what now?" David asked, spitting the words out like sand from his teeth.

Philip slowly took off the bandages and revealed his true identity as the Assistant Director of FEMA.

"My god, you are Philip Lodge," David gasped. "No wonder we were always in the gun sights of Darren, Jon, and the stooges from the corporation."

"How astute of you, David, but a little too late, and now we have all of you and the manuscript, which makes for quite a profitable day. And, when the others come down, we will have the amulet and scroll!" He laughed.

"What did you do with Ralph after he didn't die? I assume you knew he was warned about the poison?"

"Ah, it was your black friends, I suppose, who warned him. Ralph is in a cell here, a cell that he will share with you along with Olaf and your sister. I was very sorry to find out that you had recruited Ralph without telling me and placed him to spy on Darren. It is too bad he didn't die from the poison at the time. However, we have other plans for all of you now. Your deaths will give us a new opportunity to get the proverbial ball rolling toward our grand objective. We will have martyrs that died in defense of their country!"

"What about Faisal and Pianki?" Olaf asked.

"Well, as soon as they are brought down they will be taken to another cell… after we retrieve the amulet and scroll, of course," Philip said.

"And what then, you greedy monsters?" Sarah hissed.

"Well, then, my dear fiery Sarah, this underground facility will be blown up by Iranian terrorists. Unfortunately, you will all be killed while attempting to protect the facility from the terrorists with all of your might! We won't even need a prophecy for that horrible incident, I will tell the president personally of the terrible ordeal. He will be so very sorry to learn of it." He laughed.

"It will never work, Philip!" David stated.

"I beg to differ, David." He then nodded to the agents. "Take these moralistic fools to Ralph's cell and lock them up. When you get back, go see what's holding up the others. I just heard the elevator come back down."

After the agents had taken the three to Ralph's cell, Mona and Leila came silently through the door to Philip's office, both with crossbows at their sides.

Darren looked up and his mouth went agape.

"What the hell, who are you and how did you get in here? My god… is that you, Mary?"

One of the agents reached for his gun. Mary shot an arrow though his shoulder. At the same time, the three other agents came back and raised their guns to shoot. Leila shot a deadly arrow through one of them and Faisal and Pinaki shot the other two with arrows. Philip pulled out an automatic pistol from his desk drawer, threw another pistol to Darren, and they started to shoot as the Nubians put new arrows in their crossbows. Bullets bounced off the walls as they fired chaotically. They then ran toward a hallway. Mona fell and Faisal bent down and felt her pulse; she was dead. Leila shook her head sadly as Faisal and Pinaki looked at Mona lying on the cold cement floor in a pool of blood.

"Mona, paradise is in the next room and you now have the key. I am sure the Infinite Existence will have a special place for you in heaven." Faisal kissed her forehead and left.

The three remaining Nubians ran down the narrow hall that Darren and Philip had taken. Philip shot out the lights in the hallway as he ran, and it was instantly filled with inky blackness. As the Nubians followed slowly, they heard voices yelling. They were coming down from another hall. The Nubians went through a door to another dark hallway and met the three staring at them in the light as they came through a door from another lighted hallway. Before they could draw their pistols, arrows went through their bodies. Faisal and Pinaki ran through the door to the brightly lit hallway in the direction from which the agents had come. In a few minutes, they found a row of cells, one containing David and the others.

They went back to find the key to free their friends. When David and the rest got out and started leaving the area, all of the lights went out. They heard footsteps coming toward them.

"I have a feeling they have night vision goggles and can see in the dark while we can't," David murmured.

"I have a pin light, David," Leila stated as she handed him the small torch.

"I also have very good eyesight in the dark," Faisal stated as he looked toward the agents coming down the hall. "You all go ahead and I'll keep them held down."

Pinaki sighed and said, "I will stay here with Faisal as well." Ralph, Olaf, and David took AK-47's from some of the dead agents.

Olaf said, "I'll stay here, too, David; Faisal and Pinaki will need some firepower. You, Ralph, and Sarah try to find an exit and get the word out. The president must be notified immediately."

David hesitated but took Sarah by the hand and they followed the thin beam of light, walking away from the voices growing louder.

∞

As the agents came down the corridor with night vision goggles on, they spotted Faisal, Pinaki, and Olaf. Arrows and bullets flew like spiraling ravens toward the agents and two fell. The other agent opened fire. Pinaki was hit and his body was lifted up in the air then fell on the cold cement. Faisal moaned and put his hand on Pinaki's head, said some words, and stared at the other agents firing at him. Olaf fired his AK-47 and two more of the agents were blasted into the others. Faisal fired his crossbow and one more agent fell. The remaining agents ran back around a corner and Faisal and Olaf ran down another black corridor to safety.

David and the others tried to activate the elevator to leave, but it wouldn't work. They were locked in the underground facility with no exit and Philip had said that somewhere in the huge base was a bomb set to go off. They figured the half-mile long base was too huge to search for the bomb in the time they had left and decided on another strategy.

They ran toward the far end of the facility and away from the main offices. They met Olaf and Faisal as they emerged from another hallway. They all ran toward the other end of the facility, hoping that the bomb was not large enough to destroy the entire base. At the same time, Philip and Darren were nearing a small, hidden elevator. They would take it to safe ground, escaping the devastation that would occur in a few more minutes. When Darren got in the elevator, Philip shot him in the back. He then walked into the elevator and made a phone call to the president as the elevator rose toward the surface. After finishing his call, he had almost reached safe ground. He looked at Darren.

"Such are the rules of war, my friend; the less people involved in the conspiracy, the less opportunity for the truth getting out." He then stepped over the body and walked out of the elevator just as the base began to rumble. The explosion shook the ground. Philip smiled as he walked away.

∞

Immediately after Philip's call to the president, a news anchor with wind-tousled hair and wild eyes was frantically reporting the details given to her. One of the president's advisors had told her of a gigantic explosion. She said the only remains, according to her source, was a huge crater that went down into the earth over 500 yards. It was near the town of Santa Rosa, California. She stated that a news team had been dispatched from Santa Rosa to the area of the explosion.

A few minutes later, Father Dan was listening to the president talking to America about the huge explosion.

"My fellow Americans, the terrorist explosion that destroyed one of our major FEMA communication centers is unforgivable." He didn't say it was a secret underground base. "I have just been informed by telephone by Philip Lodge, Assistant Director of Homeland Security, that Iranian Muslim extremists had maliciously blown up one of our underground FEMA bases and murdered some of our wonderful and dedicated men and women, including Darren Williams, my personal counsel and friend, Jon Pierce, special counsel to the vice president, and Ralph Anderson of the Department of Defense, as well as many brave CIA agents. All of these deaths will be atoned for, I promise you. Our armed forces will be taking action immediately. I am sending our full armada of battle ships and carriers to the Persian Gulf right now. I am asking congress to declare war on Iran and will possibly be calling, depending on the severity of the problem, a federal emergency to invoke order number 11490 to protect the citizens from radical Iranian terrorists in America and the lethal harm they wish to unleash upon our citizens."

He also stated that two thirds of US forces across the world would be sent to Iran immediately. His voice, sounding sad, continued for 10 minutes, delineating the steps the US would be taking in the next few days and weeks. He told the American people that Mr. Lodge of Homeland Security had been right from the beginning about Iran and it was wonderful to have such dedicated people in charge of the security of the nation. He said that he did not take the calls from the Iranian leaders denying any involvement in the explosion.

Father Dan shuddered, figuring that Dr. Sarah Addison, her brother, David, two gentle Nubian priests, and possibly even his dear friend, Professor Faleel, were among the dead. He knew that if the president knew what really happened there in the bowels of the earth, he wouldn't be taking the action he planned. He shook his head, not wanting to believe the worst but unable to have faith in anything else.

The forged Nostradamus manuscript was in the hands of the conspirators, and he figured it would be faxed to the president in a short time. The president had a catastrophic incident that helped sustain the forged prophecies. The Assistant Homeland Security Director told the president he had witnessed the whole thing. It appeared that World War III was about to begin unless some miracle stopped it.

Father Dan contacted Bishop Bindello and the bishop met with Cardinal Giotto. They, in turn, told the pope of the whole plot. He called the president immediately with a story that contradicted what Philip Lodge had told him. A short time later, a Kushite sage-king called and told him the same thing.

∞

Prior to the president being informed by Philip Lodge about the terrorist bombing of the underground FEMA base, Farah Faleel was knocked off her feet when the underground base exploded. She turned and saw a huge ball of fire emanating from the underground facility and fell to her knees, sobbing. She ran back to where the elevator had been and looked down upon a huge, blazing hole; she knew no one could have survived the explosion in that area. She picked up her cell phone and dialed a number.

"Yes."

"Kashta, this is Farah. I have the scroll and amulet but I am afraid our brothers as well as Dr. Addison, her brother, and the others have been killed in a huge blast."

"Don't be too hasty, my dear Farah. Sometimes things are not what they seem. I am sure they will emerge safely and will stop the beginning of the war." With that, he hung up his phone and made a call to the President of the United States.

The president had just finished his speech to the nation regarding the terrorist bombing and what action he would be taking. Kashta told the identical story that the pope had already told him a few moments ago, adding credibility to the horrific tale. The president was confused as to what to do.

Farah nodded silently, wondering what Kashta planned to do. She didn't understand about the war of which he spoke because she had not heard the president speak. She looked back at the huge, gaping, burning crater with tears streaming from her eyes and started slowly walking back to her car through the yellow spring flowers that grew beside the dirt path. It was then that she saw Philip Lodge, the Assistant Director of Homeland Security. She could see that he had the Nostradamus manuscript in his hands and was laughing. She hid behind some bushes and saw him meet four men in a black car that had just entered the area. One was in a business suit and the other three were generals.

"I see you blew up the base," one of the generals stated.

"Yes. David came down with Sarah and some Nubians and we had to put them in a cell with Ralph. It was the only way to cover up our scheme. We had to make sure they said nothing. However, it added credibility to my story when I told the president about the Iranian terrorists. Those killed in the blast will be viewed as martyrs trying to save the base."

"We heard the president speaking just as we arrived here. He must have gotten on the air immediately after listening to your sad tale."

"I hope all of those trying to stop us are now dead!" the Assistant Director of the Department of Defense added.

"Yes, there is no way the ones in the facility could escape. There was only one other escape route, and that one was at the far end of the base. The only others are Catholic religious… our plan is safe."

"Well then, Philip, our plan has started. The president was very convinced. You did a wonderful job. It won't be too long now before we can unleash our weapons on the nations in the Middle East."

"Yes, General Shermak, the wheels are now in motion. I told him about the Nostradamus manuscript predicting the assassination of the Israeli ambassador. We will be able to use it soon and continue with the rest of our plan."

"Good! Now we can take over Iran and the rest of the Islamic states like we should have when we went into Iraq," General Probroudes stated. "I think we should look into taking over Russia and Venezuela sometime in the near future as well. They both have enough oil to make us even wealthier than the Middle Eastern nations. Add that oil supply to our own emerging oil supply and it will give us control over all the oil on the earth. We will be worth untold hundreds of trillions of dollars!"

The three laughed, shook hands, and left in the car. Farah couldn't believe what she had heard. She sighed and wondered what would happen now, and especially if the armament and defense power and wealth seekers could be stopped.

Epilogue

After Philip and the generals had left the bombed out area, Farah turned slowly to go to her car, still crying over the loss of her brothers and the others. She then heard muted noises and saw some umbrae walking in a haze slowly up from the far end of the destroyed underground base. In a few moments, she recognized Faisal. As they approached, she could see that all of them were covered with soot and grime, but they were alive!

"Oh, my dear Infinite Existence, how did they get out safely? And how did Kashta know?" Farah whispered to herself as she turned around and started waving and running toward the group. The survivors waved back.

∞

Five hours later, after calling the president and arriving in DC in a CIA jet, Ralph, Faisal, David, Olaf, Dr. Addison, and Dr. Faleel held a meeting with the president to explain the Nostradamus conspiracy and the use of the underground blast to cause the president to blame Iran and start a war on all Islamic nations. The president had already heard about the Nostradamus manuscript from the Vatican and a Kushite sage and now knew it had to be true.

They also told him that it was Philip Lodge who was the head of the conspiracy along with Darren Williams, Jon Pierce, and five generals. The very next hour, the president called back the fleet and cancelled the attack on Iran. He reluctantly called the president of Iran and told him it was not true that he was going to invade his country; America's armed forces were only doing practice readiness maneuvers.

Five generals were irate about not invading Iran, but escaped from the country when they heard they were going to be arrested for treason. Philip Lodge was also able to escape with the help of some senators. Others who were part of the plan but had not been identified had to obey the president's orders.

The group did not want to give up their plan to eventually invade Iran and other Middle Eastern nations in order to take over their oil, but now totally new schemes would have to be developed. The use of the forged Nostradamus manuscript was no longer a viable option. Philip Lodge, along with five generals from the Pentagon and 12 wealthy individuals in the defense, banking, and oil industries, later met in Prague to develop another option.

For now, America was safe again, at least for a short time.

About the Author

Dr. Piatt earned his BS and MA from California State Polytechnic University and his doctorate from BYU. Prior to his retirement, he was a missile engineer and launch-conductor, a science teacher and alternative high school principal, a junior college professor of psychology, engineering, and philosophy, as well as Dean. He was also a College Professor of Education and an administrator of master of education programs. He has published over 620 poems, 35 short stories, and seven essays in over 100 magazines and anthologies.

Broken Publications published his debut book of poetry *The Silent Pond* in 2012. Write Words Inc. published his debut science fiction novel *The Ideal Society* in 2012. His poetry book *Ancient Rhythms* was published by Broken Publications in 2014 and his novel *The Monk* was published in 2013, also by Broken Publications.

All of his books are available on Amazon.

www.ingramcontent.com/pod-product-compliance
Lightning Source LLC
Chambersburg PA
CBHW060217180626
46813CB00007B/2860